Wild Fae Primrose

WILD FAE PRIMROSE

COURT OF MIDSUMMER MAYHEM

BOOK 1.5

TARA GRAYCE

Wild Fae Primrose
A Court of Midsummer Mayhem Companion
Court of Midsummer Mayhem Book 1.5

LCCN: 2023914830

ISBN: 978-1-943442-36-2

N
W E
S
Court of Ice
Wilderness Court
Court of Artisans
Goblin Court
Court of Stone
Court of Islands
Court of Mists
Harvest Court
Court of Sand
Court of Grass
Faerie Market
Great Library
Court of Revels
Court of Knowledge
Tanglewood
King Oberon & Queen Titania's Court
Queen Mab's Court
Court of Dreams
Court of Jungles
Court of Seas
Queen Hippolyta's Court
Swamp Court
Court of Swordmaidens
Fae Realm

The Wild Fae Primrose

Chapter One

He had come for her at last.

Brigid froze at the pounding of hooves on the dry, hard-packed ground outside of her family's tiny hovel, an echoing drumbeat that matched her pounding pulse.

Cullen, the man who held their failing farm's debts, had come to collect. For eight months, she'd managed to put him off, using every trick she knew to buy herself time, hoping that her older sister Meg would return.

Meg wasn't coming back. Eight months ago, she had left in the night with a desperate plan to get herself snatched by a fae lord on the last-ditch hope that she could bargain for enough gold to pay off Cullen and save her siblings from indentured servitude.

She'd told them to run if she wasn't back in a year. But it had been eight months. Surely if she was coming back, she would have by now. Four more months wouldn't make a difference.

Meg was lost to them. Either she lay dead in the forest,

her body picked over by scavengers, or she had disappeared into the wildness of the Fae Realm, never to be seen again. It was what usually happened to those snatched by the fae. If they did return, it was years or decades later, with wild tales and a far wilder look in their haunted eyes.

No, Brigid was on her own. It was up to her to see to the survival of her remaining siblings.

She turned to them as the hoofbeats drew closer. Fourteen-year-old Sebastian clenched his fists as he faced the door. Beside him, thirteen-year-old Viola gripped the shoulders of their youngest sibling, ten-year-old Beatrice. All of them stared first at the door, then at Brigid, with wide eyes and white faces.

At sixteen, Brigid wasn't much older. But she was the adult right now because she had no other choice.

She drew her shoulders straighter. "Sebastian, keep Viola and Beatrice safe."

Sebastian nodded, then gestured Viola and Beatrice into the corner next to where their thin, straw pallets were stacked against the wall to keep them out of the way during the day. There wasn't anywhere else to hide in the tiny, one-room hut. There wasn't even a back door for them to dart through to escape, though Sebastian could probably kick out one of the rotting boards near the floor, given time.

They didn't have time. The hoofbeats halted outside the door with a jingle of metal and the creak of leather as the riders dismounted.

Brigid stepped into the center of the room and faced the door. She refused to back down.

Perhaps she should have taken her siblings and run, before it got to this moment. But she had been waiting in the hope that Meg would defy the odds and return from the

Fae Realm. Besides, where would they run? The entire kingdom was gripped by this drought, and they had no money to travel even if they knew where to go.

Boots stomped on the step a moment before the door was kicked open, the flimsy wood banging into the wall before sagging.

Cullen stood framed in the doorway, his smirk twisting his meticulously trimmed short beard. His blond hair slicked over his forehead while his blue eyes latched on to her. "Brigid. My patience is at an end. Do you have the money to pay your debt? Or are you prepared to fulfill your family's obligation?"

He knew very well that she didn't have the money. Hence the reason for his smirk.

Brigid crossed her arms and tried for that bland smile she'd perfected to hide her fear. "My siblings are much too young for me to leave. Come back in a few months."

Cullen's smirk twisted with a hint of a sneer. "You've claimed they were too young and you are too young for the past eight months. But I'm in luck. I've found buyers who are interested in young indentured servants. I'll be taking all of you tonight."

All of them? Brigid's fingers tightened until her nails dug into her palms in a comforting kind of pain. She had been prepared to be taken away by Cullen tonight, but she could not let him take the others. Her young sisters would be sold to who knew what kind of life. And her brother would likely be worked as hard as if he were a full-grown man.

Brigid raised her chin and marched forward. "I will go willingly. But our debt is not so large that you must sell all of us. Take me but leave my siblings."

Cullen shook his head, sauntering toward her until he

loomed over her, only inches between them. "What do you really think will happen to your siblings if I leave them here? They will starve if left on their own. I'm simply seeing to their welfare by making sure they are placed where they will be clothed and fed. I would be inhumane if I abandoned them, as your sister has apparently abandoned you."

"Leave Meg out of this." Brigid shook with the urge to smack Cullen. She knew exactly what kind of life Cullen had intended to sell her pretty, nineteen-year-old sister Meg into.

Had Meg found a better life in the Fae Realm? Likely not, given the reputation of the fae for debauched pleasures.

Brigid couldn't think about that. She could only concentrate on plotting a way to spare herself the same fate when Cullen took her away. At sixteen, she was a gangly late bloomer. Would it be enough to spare her? Or would Cullen sell her into that life anyway?

"Meg is the reason you're in this position. If she'd stayed, her indenture would have spared the rest of you. Instead, she left, and the debt falls to you to pay." Cullen gripped Brigid's arm with steel fingers, his touch sending a crawling sensation up her arm.

She refused to back down. "I am willing to pay it. But you leave my siblings alone."

"No." Cullen motioned to his men, standing just outside the door. "Grab the others."

Four men poured into the hut, crowding the tiny space. The final one closed the door behind him and stood in front of it to cut off their only means of escape.

The other three advanced on Sebastian, Viola, and Beatrice.

"No!" Brigid wrenched at her arm, trying to free herself

from Cullen. His grip tightened, and she cried out. When she tried to raise her free hand to strike him, he blocked her strike easily enough.

In the corner, Beatrice screamed and buried her face against Viola's arm. Sebastian stood in front of both of them, as if he thought he could take on all three of Cullen's goons by himself.

The door flung open again with such force that it knocked aside Cullen's man.

Meg stood there, whole and healthy, her golden-blonde hair wet and spreading damp spots onto clothes that looked clean and neat. Not like someone who had been tortured in the Fae Realm for the past eight months.

What was Meg doing here? How had she gotten here? Where was the fae lord she was supposed to have married?

There was no time for answering those questions or freezing under the shock of seeing her sister, alive and well, after so long. All cleaned up, Meg was far too pretty. The moment Cullen clapped eyes on her, he'd take her too. He'd take all of them, and Brigid had to make sure that at least one of her siblings remained free.

"Meg! You need to get out of here!" Brigid kicked Cullen's shin as hard as she could.

Cullen winced and gave a small hop as he turned to face the door.

Instead of running, Meg continued to stand there. She met Cullen's gaze unflinchingly even as he swept a sneering glance over her.

"Ah, Meg. Just in time. You are looking well. Very well." Cullen's smirk widened.

Meg lifted her chin, a hint of a smile growing on her face. "Let her go."

"Are you offering yourself in her place?" Cullen tightened his grip on Brigid's arm, squeezing so hard that she had to clench her teeth against the pain. His gaze remained locked on Meg with a devouring greediness. He didn't want her for himself. Instead, he was slavering over the money he could get by selling her. "I might get enough for you to pay your family's debt. Maybe. I have expenses, you know, and the interest for your little excuse for a farm has built up considerably. It is a pity, but I am a businessman."

Brigid blinked at the tears that pricked the corners of her eyes at the pain of his clutching fingers. She wanted to fight. Wanted to find the words to get herself out of this. Instead, all she could do was sag.

More footsteps sounded on the doorstep. What now? Who else could that be? Could this get any worse?

Strangely, Meg's smile widened until she was the one smirking. "No, you traffic in human lives under the guise of indentured servitude. But that ends today."

On the heels of Meg's words, four hard-eyed fae women wearing chain mail and carrying swords marched into the hut, followed by a dark-haired male fae in a black coat. Finally, a brown pony with a white star on his forehead and a white heart-shaped splotch on his nose stuck his head inside, his wild mane and forelock falling over his eyes. The hut was decidedly crowded now with all of them squeezed inside.

Cullen gaped, until one of the muscular fae women pressed her sword to his throat. Then he released his grip on Brigid's arm.

Her fingertips tingling as blood flowed back to her hand, Brigid dashed to Viola and Beatrice, hugging them to her. What was going on? Who were all these fae? Was that fae male the lord that Meg had set out to marry? Were these women his warriors that he was unleashing on Meg's enemies?

Surely that couldn't be it. Life didn't hold the happy endings as told in folk tales and legends.

Meg stalked to Cullen. "You will never harm my family again."

Cullen quailed, but his gaze was still shifting. Brigid swallowed at the guile she saw there.

A squeaky voice speaking unintelligible words came from the doorway a moment before a green-skinned little creature wearing nothing but a few leaves around his middle popped into the room.

Beatrice whimpered, and her arms tightened around Brigid. Viola made a noise in the back of her throat while even Sebastian took a half-step back. Brigid could only gape at the strange critter, even as Meg seemed to have a conversation with it.

Then the horse peering through the doorway spoke in that same language, his mouth moving in an unnatural, not horse-like way.

It was too much. All too much. This had to be some kind of nightmare. Maybe she really had been taken by Cullen, and this was all some kind of fantasy her tortured mind had come up with to deal with the trauma.

"What...what is that thing? What's it saying?" Cullen squeaked and backed away from the fae warrior women and the odd green creature. The creature grinned, showing off rows of white, sharp teeth, and bounded a step closer to Cullen. Cullen pressed his back to the wall. "Get it away from me!"

The creature spoke again, and Meg waved to Cullen.

Dark black-green eyes glowing and glinting, the creature advanced toward Cullen, all of his teeth on display.

Cullen gave an unmanly shriek and dashed for the door. His henchmen raced after him with the creature on their heels. A strange, inhuman cackling echoed on the night air, accompanied by very human screams.

Brigid swallowed and forced her voice to work. "Meg, what's going on? Who are all these…people?" She hated the way her voice squeaked at the end.

"It's all right. Everything is going to be all right from now on." Meg crossed the room and wrapped Brigid in a hug. She smelled clean and like something floral. Her damp hair especially wafted that scent into the night air, so different from the dirt of the hovel and Brigid's clothes.

Brigid herself smelled of the earth and hard work. She couldn't remember the last time they'd had enough water for a true bath.

"You were gone for so long." Beatrice changed her hug from Brigid to Meg, bursting into tears.

"We thought you were never coming back." Viola launched herself into the hug, wrapping her arms around both Meg and Beatrice.

"How long was I gone?" Meg glanced between them, as if she didn't know how long it had been.

"Eight months." Sebastian was blinking rapidly as if to hide his own emotions at the return of their sister.

Meg drew in a deep breath, as if to absorb that news. Then, she seemed to pull herself together, the smile returning, as she glanced between Viola and Beatrice. "I'm here now. And you're all going to be safe." Meg glanced over her shoulder, sharing a smile with the handsome fae male.

Brigid stared at Meg. Something hot and wet trickled

down her cheeks. After all these months of being on her own, of thinking that Meg was gone forever, and yet here her sister was, healthy and seemingly unaffected by her time in the Fae Realm.

But she couldn't trust how good this looked. The fae male had chiseled features, dark brown hair that fell over his forehead, and chocolate-brown eyes. He was handsome and beautiful in that fae way, and surely that made him dangerous. Had he bewitched Meg somehow? Was he trying to trick the rest of them somehow by using Meg?

Brigid lowered her voice and leaned closer to Meg. "Is that the fae lord you set out to marry? Is he going to pay off Cullen with faerie gold as you hoped?"

If he didn't, then this would all be for nothing. Cullen would be scared off for a night, but he would be back. And a fae lord wasn't about to camp out in their hut waiting to chase him off again.

Sebastian crossed his arms and glared at the fae lord. "Does he treat you right?"

Meg reached out and rested a hand on Sebastian's shoulder, waiting until he looked at her. "Basil has been very good to me. The best, actually."

Was that the truth? Or had this Basil tricked her somehow? Was being nice to her all part of an elaborate game?

Meg turned and gestured to the fae male. "Everyone, this is my husband, Basil. He's a Master Librarian at a magic library."

What kind of job was Master Librarian? Was he a fae lord?

The fae male, Basil, lifted his hand and gave a little wave and a smile, but he didn't speak. Why not? Should Brigid find that suspicious?

The shaggy pony snorted. Meg grinned and gestured to him. "And this is Buddy. I mean, Sir Buddy the Magnificent. He is our talking pony companion and the most valiant steed I know."

Now Brigid knew her sister had been fae-glamoured out of her mind. Her sister didn't talk with such pompous words.

Meg's arms tightened around them as her smile widened. "Basil has offered to do even better than pay off Cullen. We're taking all of you back to the Fae Realm to live with us."

Now Brigid was positive this had to be some kind of trick. Why would Basil want all of them? He had to want them for some nefarious reason, and he was using Meg to get them.

But what other choice did they have? The moment Cullen escaped that little green fae monster, he would be back, and he would be angry for being chased off in such a manner. He would take all of them, and he would split them apart and sell them. She would never see any of her siblings again.

It didn't matter why Basil wanted them or what would happen to them in the Fae Realm. At least, if they went with Meg, they would be together to face whatever twisted torments the Fae Realm had in store for them.

The talking pony Buddy and the four warrior women—swordmaidens, as Meg and Basil called them—stepped outside. Perhaps to give them a moment to pack and say goodbye to their old life. Or maybe to lull them into a false sense of security by pretending kindness.

As soon as they were alone, Brigid tried to take Meg aside. Perhaps if they broke through the boards in the rear of the hut, they still had a chance to sneak away from the fae. Meg didn't have to return with that fae, did she?

But Meg didn't listen, and soon their siblings had pulled her away to help with packing, their excited chatter filling the space where fear had been before.

Packing their meager belongings took little time. They took a few mementos of their parents—a quilt their mother had made of their father's shirts, a worn dress of their mother's, a wooden doll their mother had fashioned for Beatrice—but there was little else worth taking. Meg assured them they wouldn't need the rags they called clothes or bedding or their cracked wooden bowls and dented pewter cup that they had to share between them.

Brigid swallowed as she stared at the sparse, empty hut for the last time. It wasn't much, but it was home. It was theirs.

Except that it wasn't theirs. They had mortgaged it to Cullen, and since they didn't have the money they owed and they didn't intend to let him sell them into indentured servitude, the farm belonged to Cullen. Every withered cornstalk and speck of parched dirt was now his.

There was nothing left for them here but slavery and separation.

Would the Fae Realm be any better? Were they just trading slavery here for slavery there?

Meg glanced around at each of them before she turned to her fae captor-husband Basil. "We're ready."

Basil pushed away from the wall, then he grimaced, his mouth tight and his face going gray even with his bronzed complexion.

Meg hurried to his side and looped his arm over her

shoulder. "You shouldn't have been up so soon. You should be resting."

Basil leaned against her, the look in his chocolate-brown eyes warm as he looked down at Meg. He spoke into Meg's ear, too low for Brigid to hear.

Brigid shifted, something in his expression too sincere and tender for her liking. This Basil couldn't possibly *love* Meg, could he? He was fae. And he'd stolen Meg from her realm. No fae who snatched a human could have good motives for doing so.

Even if Meg had gone into the forest hoping to be snatched. That still didn't make it all right in Brigid's book. Especially since Basil had kept her away so long.

Beatrice, clutching her doll to her chest, leaned closer to Meg. "Is he all right?"

Meg nodded as she took Beatrice's hand. "Yes. Just a small disagreement with a basilisk. But don't worry. Basil was very heroic."

Basil snorted but he didn't say anything.

Sebastian's eyes brightened. "Will I get to learn to fight in the Fae Realm?"

Viola swerved closer to him. "It sounds scary."

Brigid swallowed and gripped her sack of meager belongings tighter. It did sound scary. And dangerous. More dangerous even than staying here with the threat of Cullen looming over them. Why did Meg think this was a good idea?

Meg's smile dimmed, and she glanced between each of them before her gaze landed on Brigid and stayed there. "I'm not going to lie to you. The Fae Realm is dangerous. There are monsters that wander in from the Realm of Monsters and cause trouble. And the other fae can be a bit dangerous as well. But we'll figure out ways to keep you all safe. Sebastian, I'm not sure if Queen Hippolyta and her swordmaidens will agree to train you since you're a boy, but everyone who works at the Great Library at least gets a club and some training in how to fight."

Still leaning heavily on Meg, Basil met Sebastian's gaze with a tentative look of his own and gave a slight nod. "I can teach you."

Basil's voice was a high baritone, and he spoke softly, as if he was afraid of scaring them off.

Sebastian pumped his fist. "Yes!"

Buddy, the talking pony, stuck his head back inside and tilted his nose toward the night outside. He spoke, his mouth moving in that oddly human way, though Brigid couldn't understand him.

Huh. Why could she understand Basil, but not the pony? What was going on?

"Right." Meg stepped forward, all but dragging both Basil and Beatrice along with her. "Come on, everyone. We're going home."

It was the second time Meg had called the Fae Realm home, and it sent a prickling dread down Brigid's spine. How could Meg use a word like *home* to describe the Fae Realm and her life with her fae kidnapper?

As they stepped out of their tiny hut for the last time, Brigid couldn't help but turn and shut the door, even if there was no reason to try to keep the critters and elements out of the hovel. It was such an automatic gesture. But it was also a farewell, of sorts. A farewell to this house. This life. This realm.

Buddy knelt on one knee and said something while looking at Basil.

Basil shook his head and gestured to Beatrice, then Viola. "Meg's sisters can ride. I'm fine."

Beatrice grinned, let go of Meg's hand, and raced over to Buddy. She flopped against his neck since she couldn't boost herself on even with Buddy kneeling. "I'd love to ride!"

Meg sent Basil a roll of her eyes that seemed to be directed at him for refusing to ride, then she helped first Beatrice, then Viola, onto Buddy's back.

Once they were situated, two of the swordmaidens led the way into the nearby forest.

Well, it wasn't much of a forest. Many of the trees had withered and died in the drought. Some had fallen, turning the forest into a twisting maze of dead, tangled branches. No undergrowth remained, as it had all died or been eaten by desperate, hungry animals long ago.

Buddy, with Beatrice and Viola giggling as they clung to his back, followed the swordmaidens with Meg still supporting Basil stumbling after them. Sebastian marched in their wake as if eager to reach the Fae Realm and his promised sword lessons.

As if the fae would actually teach him how to use a sword that he could someday use against them.

Brigid trudged in the rear with the final two swordmaidens at her heels as if to make sure she didn't get second thoughts and run before they had a chance to get her into their realm.

Only a sliver of moon hanging low in the sky lit their way, creating sinister silhouettes of the nearly naked branches overhead.

The circle of stones bordered by trees came into view,

and the back of Brigid's neck prickled. The faerie circle. Once they stepped through, there would be no going back.

Basil turned, still leaning on Meg. "Hold on to Buddy as we go through the circle. We don't want to get separated, and talking pony companions are even better at navigating fae circles than we fae are."

The two swordmaidens in the lead had already rested their hands on Buddy's neck. Meg and Basil crowded close, and Meg even twined her fingers in Buddy's mane.

With nothing else for it, Brigid stepped close and buried her fingers in the sleek hair of Buddy's rump.

When everyone was holding on to Buddy, the pony stepped into the faerie circle, and they all had to shuffle along with him.

Then he took another step, and the whole world tilted. Brigid tried to take a breath, but it caught in her chest as something heavy and light all at the same time squeezed her chest—her whole body—as if grinding her into dust.

Lights swirled through the haze of her vision, and she caught glimpses of things through the haze. Dunes of sand. A giant lizard-looking creature—a dragon—curled amongst rocks. Icy winds sweeping down mountains as gray-skinned rock creatures trundled through the drifts. A field of pumpkins guarded by a scarecrow that shuffled around on straw legs and scratched at the top of his pumpkin head.

A sweet, luring sort of tugging drew her forward, as if the realm itself was grasping her by the hand and tempting her to its wild wonders.

Then Buddy took another step, and the world righted itself with a snap that would've sent Brigid to her knees if she hadn't been so tightly gripping Buddy's hair.

She gulped in a deep breath of the strangely thick air of this world.

They now stood in a forest so very unlike the one they'd left behind that Brigid blinked. A late afternoon sun now gleamed in the sky above them, lighting every twisting vine and shaggy piece of moss dangling from the twisting branches of the large, squat trees surrounding them. The ground below them was covered in spongy moss while tiny red flowers grew in clumps around them.

Buddy snorted, then shook his head, making the strands of his mane that weren't tightly gripped in someone's hand shake. "You can all stop clutching me so tightly. We're here."

Viola blinked and patted Buddy's shoulder from her place on his back. "Why can I suddenly understand you?"

Basil steadied himself with a hand on Buddy and his other arm still looped around Meg while he glanced up at Viola. "The binding to the Court has already begun since you went with us willingly. You can now understand the fae, a necessity so that you can knowledgeably complete the binding."

Finish the binding. That sounded ominous. But what other choice did they have?

"Why could we understand you before, but we couldn't understand Buddy?" Brigid glanced from Basil to the pony and back. It seemed rather important to understand just what was going on.

"I'm married to a human. The binding gives me the ability to communicate in the Human Realm." Basil smiled down at Meg, and she returned his smile.

"I wasn't sure if it would work." Meg gave a small shrug and reached up to rest her hand over Basil's on her shoulder.

Such a normal, romantic gesture. But was it real? Or had Basil ensnared Meg somehow, perhaps to gain this binding that he spoke of?

Brigid looked away from him and down at the little red flowers growing between the moss. They almost looked like the tiny wildflowers that grew at home, though she couldn't remember their name.

The little reminder of home ached inside her chest. Would she ever see the wildflowers of the Human Realm again?

Or would she be stuck here, captive to the whims of this Basil?

Chapter Two

Brigid stared around them as they strolled along the moss-covered trail that extended from the forest to the great white palace that perched on the hill. The moss was soft and springy beneath her bare feet, a change from the hard-packed ground of the realm she'd left behind. A crystalline river—far more clear and turquoise than anything Brigid had ever seen in the Human Realm—ran along the base of the castle before cascading down a short waterfall to meander between the houses of the small village surrounding the castle.

Along one side of the river, great mansions perched among lush gardens and mini forests. On the near side of the river, quaint stone houses with thatched roofs appeared almost like a village found in the Human Realm, except for the fact that it was all too neat and picturesque.

Not to mention that strange people of every shape, size, and color from bright blue to leafy to purple-skinned walked through the village and up to the castle on the hill.

"That's King Theseus's castle on the left. The Great

Library is on the right, and they are connected by the Hall of Anywhere Doors." Basil's voice lifted with something almost like pride as he gestured at the castle and Library ahead of them.

Everything was so green and lush. So unlike the drought-dead land they'd left behind.

As they climbed the causeway that led up to the large gates of the castle, Basil's face paled still further, and he pressed a hand to his side.

Meg tugged his arm more firmly over her shoulders. "You should be resting."

"I will soon. But we need to get your family bound to the court as soon as possible. It's dangerous to leave a binding half-done, and especially dangerous for humans to wander the Fae Realm unbound." Basil straightened a bit, as if to prove to Meg that he was fine. "I'll rest once we know your family will be safe."

Brigid resisted the urge to snort. Basil sounded so sincere. Surely he didn't mean it. Maybe he just wanted to make sure they were bound to him as soon as possible before they realized how bad of an idea it was.

"All right." Meg adjusted her grip on him. "But we're taking the Anywhere Door back to the House. No more walking for you if we can help it."

"I heartily agree to that." Basil steadied himself against Buddy's neck. "I'm not sure how long we'll have to wait before King Theseus has a moment to see us since he and Queen Hippolyta are probably still caught up in celebrations. Most weddings in the Fae Realm are a private affair, but the wedding of monarchs is a big deal. There are a lot of festivities today."

"There was quite the hubbub already when we left." Meg

shrugged. "Though most of that was caused by everyone trying to clean up the mess the monsters left behind before the festivities got started in earnest."

Their escort led the way through the double doors into the castle, and all of them stepped into a massive room made entirely of white marble. Columns supported the arched ceiling while doors were set into the walls between each of the pillars.

Most eye-catching were all the fae bustling through the halls and in and out of the doors. Many of the fae were like Basil—looking much like humans, except for their tapered ears and extraordinary beauty.

But others…those made Brigid want to duck outside and hide. Tall, tree-like creatures shuffled along on trunk-like legs and roots for toes, their arms waving like branches as leaves fluttered around their heads. Tiny sparkles flitted around the trees before darting off while other short critters with skin in all the tones of green, blue, and purple hopped between other fae. Some fae had fur and animalistic features. Others were so strange that Brigid couldn't even comprehend what she was seeing.

Yet the clothes they were wearing arrested her attention. Woven leaf skirts and flower petal dresses. Silks so vibrant and shimmering that they flowed like water when the fae moved. Brigid's fingers itched to touch fabric that fine.

Basil gestured around him. "Welcome to the Great Hall of Anywhere Doors. These doors connect to all of the courts in the Fae Realm so that everyone can visit the Court of Knowledge and its Great Library, seeking the knowledge we provide. We also have outpost libraries in some of the other courts to better serve the fae living there."

Meg elbowed him. "Basil, don't use up all your lecturing in one go."

Basil paused and glanced down at Meg, giving her a sheepish kind of smile. "Right. Come on, everyone."

He led the way down the center of the hall, occasionally lifting his hand and greeting one of the other fae.

At the far end of the hall, ornate double doors were set between larger pillars. Two of the intimidating fae warrior women stood in front of the door, gripping spears as tall as they were and glaring down at anyone who came close.

But the doors had been flung open, and the fae women didn't stop anyone from coming or going.

Meg glanced over her shoulder as they walked into what appeared to be the entry hall of a castle. "The swordmaidens are from Queen Hippolyta's court. She's the Queen of the Court of Swordmaidens. Since she married King Theseus, the Court of Knowledge has an agreement with the Court of Swordmaidens that they will protect our court, especially the Great Library."

Basil grinned at her. "Now I have you started on the lectures."

Meg rolled her eyes. "Grumpy groundhogs, you're right."

Together, they stepped into the bustling chaos of the castle's entry hall. It was entirely made of white marble with another set of double doors to their right, and an arched opening to a ballroom to their left. Before them, broad stairs, also of marble, rose upward.

Fae of all kinds strode about, carrying plates of food, talking in groups, or hurrying off on some unknown errand. The ballroom swirled with dancers in a whirl of color and music unlike anything Brigid had ever seen or heard.

An elderly man with a long white beard and wearing a black coat like Basil's, though this coat had gold embroidery around the cuffs and collar rather than Basil's silver, strode up to them, carrying a plate piled high with something that looked like cheese, but it was a bright green. "Basil. I see you retrieved Meg's family."

"Yes. Is King Theseus free?" Basil glanced around, but he didn't seem to see the person he was looking for.

The elderly librarian nodded and waved toward the ballroom. "The king and queen were accepting congratulations in there. You'd better hurry. The plays are about to start."

"Thank you." Basil waved in return, then he and Meg led the way into the ballroom.

Brigid couldn't wrap her mind around the sights, the people, the smells. It was all so new and different and *weird*.

A beautiful fae woman with a crown perched on her blonde hair and wearing a dress fashioned of chain mail and silk stood next to a dark-haired fae man, a crown on his head as well. Instead of a line to greet them, fae ducked out of the party, greeted them, then returned to the party without missing a beat.

Buddy clopped into the ballroom, forging a path through the milling, dancing fae for the rest of them to follow. Even though he was only a pony, he was still large enough that the fae dodged out of his way.

As they reached the fae king and queen, Buddy tipped his head in a pony bow. Basil and Meg dipped into as much of a bow as they could manage while Meg was supporting Basil.

Brigid wasn't sure what to do. Was she supposed to bow or curtsy or what? She was a poor girl from a farm. She didn't know anything about curtsying.

King Theseus smiled, adding grooves to his thin face. "Master Librarian Basil. It appears that you retrieved your family."

"Yes, thank you." Basil tipped his head to Queen Hippolyta. "And especially thank you, Your Majesty, for your swordmaiden escort. They proved very helpful."

"Swordmaidens usually are." Queen Hippolyta smiled up at her husband with a little twist of her lips that spoke of a running joke between them.

King Theseus reached for her hand, then turned to them. "As I promised, I will bind your family to our court. Has the binding been explained to them?"

Basil shook his head. "We thought it best to come straight here."

"Wise, considering the chaos of last night." King Theseus glanced between each of them, and his brown eyes held a warm compassion that was a sharp contrast with the cool assessment in his wife's eyes.

Brigid shifted under their scrutiny, all the more aware of her bare, dirty feet, grungy dress, tangled hair, and body that hadn't been washed in far too long, given the lack of water for drinking, much less for bathing.

King Theseus clasped his hands behind his back. "Once you are bound to the Court of Knowledge, you will be afforded all the rights and privileges of any fae of my court. You will be provided with a home, food, clothing, and work at the Great Library under Master Librarian Basil and Assistant Librarian Meg."

Was that the reason Basil had snatched Meg, and now them? He wanted help in this Great Library they all kept mentioning.

"The binding will give you the same protections as any

member of my court." King Theseus smiled at each of them. "Who would like to go first?"

Sebastian started forward, but Brigid lunged and gripped his arm, halting him. She glanced around at her siblings, wishing she could speak with them alone for a few moments. But it seemed their fae captors wouldn't allow that. "Are we sure about this? This doesn't seem safe."

It went against everything their mother had always taught them. Stay away from the forest. Stay away from fae.

Meg touched Brigid's arm and met her gaze. "It's safe, Brigid."

Brigid lowered her voice, whispering in a tone she hoped the fae in the room couldn't hear, "We can't trust them. All their kindness is just an act. That's how the fae are."

"Not these fae. Their kindness is real. Basil is the kindest person I've ever met, fae or human." Meg's brown eyes pleaded with Brigid to believe her. "He will be a big brother to all of you, if you let him."

"I don't need a big brother." The words snapped out before she thought them through, but she refused to take them back or regret them. Even as pain twisted Meg's features and that fae, Basil, hunched a bit as if he'd been punched. All an act, surely. He was fae. He couldn't actually *want* to be a part of their family.

"Brigid..." Meg still hadn't let go of Brigid's arm, even if her grip was now tight, her eyes pained.

"I don't want a big brother." Brigid kept her chin up, refusing to back down. This was her last chance to talk her family out of this. Even if having this out in front of the fae was far from ideal. "I want my big sister back."

"I *am* back." Meg gave Brigid's arm a small shake. "I

wouldn't bring our family here if I didn't believe this was the best thing for us. For *all* of us."

Was this the best thing for their family?

Perhaps it was. All that was left for them back in the Human Realm was being sold by Cullen, separated from each other, and the slow death of life in the slavery of indentured servitude.

But was this life any better? Was Meg in her right mind? Or was she glamoured out of her senses?

Did it matter? Meg was clean, well-fed, and well-dressed. Was it worth losing one's mind and autonomy to gain that?

What was Brigid supposed to do? Even she knew enough about the Fae Realm to know it was too dangerous to remain as they were and refuse the binding to the Court.

The fae king and queen remained silent, as did Basil. Strange, that they weren't trying to lure Brigid to their side. Or, perhaps, they knew they could afford to stay silent. What choice did she have—did any of them have—in the end?

Sebastian glanced between Brigid and Meg before he pulled his arm free. "Meg's never let us down. If she says it's safe, then it's safe."

With that, he stepped forward, as if utterly unworried about the ramifications of just blindly agreeing to this binding.

"Kneel and hold out your hand. I will rest my hand on yours, and say, 'I claim you for my court.' You will then answer, 'I accept your claim.' Understand?" King Theseus held Sebastian's gaze.

It all sounded rather...permanent. Once they were

bound to the Court, would they become as glamoured and accommodating as Meg?

But Brigid could only watch helplessly as Sebastian nodded, then knelt and extended his hand, despite Brigid's objections and their mother's warnings.

King Theseus touched the back of his hand, and a glow surrounded their hands. A weight of magic gathered around them, so thick that a human like Brigid could sense it.

Sebastian flinched, but he didn't pull away. Instead he held the fae king's gaze fearlessly.

"I claim you for my court."

Sebastian lifted his chin. "I accept your claim."

The gathering magic settled around them, then flashed once. The glow around their hands vanished in a blink.

"Welcome to the Court of Knowledge." King Theseus tipped his head with a slight smile.

Viola went next, then Beatrice.

Then it was Brigid's turn. She hesitated, staring at the space before King Theseus. What was she supposed to do?

Did she really have a choice? At this point, there was nothing for it but to let the king claim her and join her family in whatever future the Fae Realm held.

She drew in a deep breath, stepped forward, and knelt in front of King Theseus.

In moments, it was done. She repeated the words, the binding settled around her, and she was bound to the Court of Knowledge, come what may.

She didn't feel any different as the magic of the binding settled on her. Her thoughts didn't turn fuzzy, and she didn't gain an instant, uncontrolled admiration for the fae king and queen.

No, she felt like herself. But would she feel any different if she were glamoured? Would she be able to tell?

As she stood, a fae man with donkey ears bounded up to them. "King Theseus, Queen Hippolyta, my players are ready to put on our performance to celebrate your marriage."

King Theseus nodded. "Thank you. We will be there shortly." The fae king gestured to them. "You are all welcome to attend the play. You are members of the court now."

"Do say you'll come, Basil!" The donkey-headed man turned to Basil, an imploring look on his donkey-esque face. "And Meg! And…"

"This is my family." Meg gestured to them, then her smile faded. "We'd love to come, but Basil—"

"Of course we'll come." Basil met Meg's gaze.

"Basil…" Meg drew out his name, gesturing vaguely at his side where he'd been wounded.

"I'm fine." Basil pushed himself a little straighter as if to prove his words true. "Your family will enjoy witnessing this performance."

"I suppose…" Meg sighed and nodded. "All right. We'll go. But then we are getting you straight back to the House afterwards. No arguments. A tour of the Great Library can wait until tomorrow."

The House? The way Meg said the word sounded more like a name than merely a *house* the way they would say it back in the Human Realm.

The play turned out to be…strange. A tragedy that was played with such frivolity that it seemed more like a comedy, and even Brigid hadn't been able to help but laugh.

The House was even stranger than the play. The

moment they stepped through the magical Anywhere Door —doors that acted like portals between two points—the grumpy, semi-sentient House had forced them all to take baths.

The bath in the warm water of the grotto with an array of scented soaps had been pleasant. And when Brigid had opened the door to what Meg claimed was her room, Brigid found a floofy, swirly dress waiting for her in the wardrobe. If Basil and his House were trying to bribe her into letting her guard down, it was starting to work.

It had worked on the rest of Brigid's family. Couldn't they see how dangerous Basil likely was? All this kindness couldn't be trusted. But none of them were listening when Brigid warned them. She would just have to be wary for all of them.

A play in the Fae Realm. A House. All of it was so strange. So new.

And so very, very dangerous.

Chapter Three

Brigid snuggled deeper into the moss-covered nook that served as a bed in this fae House. A soft blanket spread over her while a few flowers had sprouted from the mossy floor. A room beyond her wildest dreams. Too good to be true.

She would just have to remain wary and watch for any signs that Basil was about to unleash his nefarious scheme.

With a lurch, the moss bed tipped and dumped her onto the floor. It didn't hurt, thanks to the sponginess of the moss covering the floor. But it was still abrupt to go from the first wakeful haziness to being dropped on the floor like a sack of potatoes.

"I'm up, I'm up, you crazy House." Living inside of a House that could move and think would take some getting used to.

Brigid brushed herself off and straightened the soft nightdress she'd worn to bed.

Would that fancy, pretty dress still be in the wardrobe this morning?

She hurried across the room and flung open the wavy front to the wardrobe built into the wall.

There, the light pink, frilly dress hung where it had the night before, a perfection of ruffles and embroidery and soft silk that fell to her mid-calf. Matching silver sandals with a hint of a heel and a pink shimmer when the light caught them rested beneath the dress in the wardrobe.

She never would have worn a dress like this in the Human Realm. Her family never could have afforded it, nor would it have been wise on the farm. The farm was a place for serviceable, sturdy dresses.

It almost felt wrong to put on such a dress. Should she refuse to wear anything provided by the fae and his magical House? Would it mean giving in, letting down her guard, succumbing to the enchantment?

But the House had stolen her old clothes. She didn't have much of a choice. Not really.

Still, Brigid hesitated. It felt like a betrayal of her upbringing as a sensible farmgirl. Shouldn't she want something more practical? The clothes Meg had been wearing last night had been a good quality but still a practical brown-and-green dress with knee-high boots. If Brigid wore this dress, would she be turning her back on where she came from?

How she wanted to wear this dress. It was the most beautiful dress she'd ever seen, besides the ones worn by many of the fae the previous night.

Brigid straightened her shoulders. Why shouldn't she wear this dress? She was a member of the Court of Knowledge. Just because she wore the dress and played the part didn't mean that she was giving in. It just meant that she was canny enough to play along until she figured out the rules of this new game her family played.

The dress fell around her in soft ruffles. She smoothed it with her fingers and took in the sight of herself in the mirror. Clean, with her hair falling in a lighter blonde than she realized she possessed under the layers of grease and dirt, she looked far prettier than she had back in the Human Realm. It was a good thing Cullen couldn't see her now, or he'd start counting how much more he could get for her indenture.

She headed for the door. An Anywhere Door.

All Brigid had to do was think about where she wanted to go, and the Door would open to that location. At least, that was how it worked, in theory. Considering this particular Anywhere Door was connected to the grumpy House, it could lead wherever the House deemed it necessary for her to go.

With a deep breath, Brigid rested her hand on the latch and hoped the Door led to the main room.

When she swung it open, it did indeed lead to the main room of the House. Meg was already there, bustling around the cupboard in the kitchen, taking out food and setting it on the table. Viola and Sebastian sat at the table, gaping at the strange-colored food.

Brigid took a step into the room, and the Anywhere Door swung shut behind her, as if to make sure she couldn't run.

Only once she stood on the moss carpet did she notice that the sneaky fae Basil lounged in one of the overstuffed chairs in front of the fireplace. Lazing about while her sister did all the work.

Was that why he'd snatched Meg—and later the rest of them? He wanted human captives to serve him?

The Anywhere Door behind Brigid opened, and Beatrice spilled into the room wearing a frothy light blue dress with ruffles all along the skirt and the bodice much like Brigid's. Beatrice shoved Brigid's back. "Stop hogging the doorway. Is Buddy awake?"

The top half of the door that led to the stable swung open, and Buddy, the talking pony, stuck his head into the room, blinking sleepily at them. "Of course I'm awake. How could I sleep with all of you nattering on in here? I need my sleep after the excursion to rescue you lot."

Beatrice grinned, flounced across the room, and flung her arms around Buddy's neck. "But you still love us, don't you?"

Buddy tucked his long nose against Beatrice's back in a pony version of a hug. "Yes, of course I do."

Brigid resisted the urge to roll her eyes. The talking pony soaked up all the love Beatrice was lavishing on him.

Meg set another tray on the table, still smiling. "Breakfast is ready."

Beatrice kissed the heart-shaped splotch on Buddy's nose, then hurried to the table and plopped into a chair beside Viola.

Basil pushed to his feet and braced himself against the chair for a moment, pressing a hand to his waist.

"Basil?" Meg took a step away from the table, her smile falling away into scrunched eyebrows and a frown.

"I'm fine." Basil straightened and strode to the table, sinking into the seat at the head. "The wound is almost healed."

The wound Basil and Meg claimed he had gotten from a

monster called a basilisk. What kind of dangerous place had Meg taken them to?

Meg's frown remained as she took the seat to Basil's right. Leaving the final seat—the seat to Basil's left—for Brigid.

Brigid forced herself to walk across the room and sit at the table. As if they were having a nice, family dinner and not a meal presided over by their fae captor. She took in the spread of food and grimaced. "Is this safe to eat?"

All the food on the table was bright, weird colors. From pink toast to a vibrant green-and-purple fruit, it did not look safe. Or normal.

Basil glanced over the food, then nodded. "Yes. It doesn't appear that the House has tried to slip in any faerie fruit. This is all safe, now that King Theseus has bound you to the Court."

Brigid resisted the urge to shudder. Bound to the court. She still wasn't sure it had been the best idea, even if it had been her only option.

But Meg didn't seem to question her fae husband Basil. She just went along with everything as if she thought this was all a good thing. A happy ending.

Beatrice dug in first, exclaiming a moment later over how good the food tasted. That prompted Viola and Sebastian to dig in.

Brigid still hesitated. If she ate the food, would that start the fae glamour? Was that what had happened to her normally sensible sister Meg?

But what other choice did she have? She couldn't just not eat the food. She'd starve.

She'd always heard the faerie fruit was the most danger-ous, so she stuck to the pink toast and the green eggs. The toast was oddly sweet while the eggs had a strange tartness to them. But it was all delicious and far more food than she'd had in a long time.

Brigid only half-listened to her siblings as they chattered over breakfast. Big smiles, happy voices, bright laughter. Already so at home in this strange place, entirely unworried about the danger they were likely in.

After shoveling her last bite into her mouth, Meg pushed away from the table and shrugged into a green coat. "I can't wait to show you the Great Library. I'm afraid it might look a little rough around the edges today after all the monster attacks."

"It recovers quickly." Basil also pushed from the table, picked up his formal-looking black coat, and started to shove his arm into one of the sleeves, wincing a bit.

Meg hurried to his side and helped him. Once the coat settled on his shoulders, she smoothed the lapels and gazed up at Basil with such a tender look that Brigid had to look away.

Meg couldn't possibly be in *love* with Basil, could she? He was one of the sneaky, evil, human-snatching fae. Meg wouldn't have let down her guard and actually fallen in love with her kidnapper.

Would she?

Brigid trudged after the rest of her siblings as Basil and Meg led the way to the Anywhere Door. She had to all but peel Beatrice away from her goodbye with Buddy.

Buddy snorted, mumbled something that might have been a wish for them to have a good day, then retreated back into his stall. Probably to get more sleep.

Basil rested a hand on the latch and opened the Door to reveal the white marble hall filled with all the doors. All of them trooped through, joining the bustle of fae that was only mildly subdued from the party of the night before. This time, instead of heading toward the doors that led to the castle, the fae were lining up in front of the other set of double doors, where two swordmaidens stopped them before allowing them entry.

Basil bypassed the line and waved to one of the swordmaidens, an imposing woman with curving horns, soft cow ears, and big brown eyes. "Good morning, Minnie. They're with me."

The swordmaiden nodded to them, then opened the door.

With an eager bounce to his step, Basil led the way through the door. Beaming with pride as if he owned the place, he swept his arm in a gesture to encompass the space around them. "Welcome to the Great Library of the Court of Knowledge."

Around them, shelves upon shelves of books wound and twisted in a maze as far as Brigid could see. Above them, a glass dome arched high overhead, sunlight pouring inside. Beneath the dome, a giant tree spread its branches over the shelves, its broad leaves blocking the sunlight from touching the books and casting a hazy green light over the library. The floor was covered with moss while branches, leaves, and even flowers grew from the twisting shelves.

At the base of the giant tree, fae wearing black coats like Basil's sat at surprisingly normal looking desks while fae from the entrance lined up in front of the desks. Fae wearing green coats like Meg's bustled about, carrying stacks of books.

Off to one side, several fae in either green or black coats clustered around a blackened section of moss. Stacks of ripped and torn books were piled to the side while the fae wrestled with the splinters of what had once been shelving.

"What happened over there?" Viola pointed at the section of devastation in the otherwise peaceful and beautiful library.

"That was caused by the monster attacks last night." Meg shuddered and grimaced. "Thankfully, it seems to be all over. Though, shouldn't the Library fix itself?"

"It will. But with this much destruction, the Library needs a bit of a helping hand." Basil shrugged, then started in that direction. "They could probably use our help. It's something you and your siblings can do without knowing how to read."

Meg nodded. "That's a whole bunch of beat-up books for us to tackle."

Brigid gazed around as Meg and Basil led the way across the broad expanse of the Great Library's center atrium. This place was...wondrous. Weird. Beyond anything she could have imagined.

As they strode by, a few of the fae halted what they were doing and leaned closer to their neighbors. Whispers of "humans" and "bound to the court" nipped at Brigid's heels as she made sure Beatrice didn't dawdle.

Something blue and scaly slithered across their path. Viola yelped and stumbled back into Brigid. "What *is* that?"

The creature halted, raising its head and spreading a leathery ruff as its sharp-toothed mouth gaped at them.

Meg glanced over her shoulder, then turned back to them. She knelt and held out her hand to the creature. It slithered over to her and rubbed its head against her hand, making a sound somewhere between a purr and a growl. "This little biter is a bookwyrm. They protect the Great

Library from pests, and they help protect the books. I'm told larger bookwyrms guard the towers filled with the really dangerous books, but only Master Librarians like Basil are allowed up there." She swiveled to look up at Basil. "I guess that means you can visit the towers now."

"And I can sneak you in for a tour, if you'd like." Basil's mouth quirked.

Meg shuddered. "Maybe not right away. I'm just getting used to the little ones. I'm not ready for one of the great wyrms yet."

The same black-coated fae with white hair and a long white beard from the night before strode toward them. "Basil, I see you are punctual as always. You didn't need to come in today. Not after you were wounded yesterday."

Basil shrugged. "I wanted to see to the Library. I couldn't stay away. And I wanted to show Meg's family around."

"Good, good." The fae nodded again. "Show them around, then report to me. I'll show you to your new desk and give you a list of your new duties."

Basil's grin grew as the older fae bustled off again. "That's Head Librarian Marco. He's my boss. Well, Meg's too. Yours as well. You all will be working at the Library with us. Until you earn a librarian coat, you'll be apprentice librarians."

"As opposed to me. I'm an assistant librarian." Meg tugged on her green coat. "Just got suited up proper last night before we fetched all of you."

What kind of horrible things would the Library need them to do? Did they need to dust all the rows of shelves? Give those bookwyrms baths? Fix all this broken shelving and damaged books?

Or worse? Brigid shuddered, remembering some of the

darker tales she'd heard about the fae. Tales of them snatching humans for dark rituals, feeding their magic with blood.

Did this Great Library need blood to water its tree and moss? Would it work the life out of them, then consume them when they had served their purpose?

Brigid remained silent and wary as Basil showed them around the maze of shelves, pointing at various rooms and spouting off information as if any of them cared.

Perhaps a few of them did. By the time they ended their tour, Beatrice was toting around one of the yellow book-wyrms, scratching behind its ruff, while Viola gazed about with growing wonder. Even Sebastian had begun nodding along.

Didn't any of them see the danger? Surely Basil was just luring them into a false sense of security.

Once the tour was over, the real work began, as Brigid had known it would. While Basil went off to do who knew what with Head Librarian Marco—probably plotting the blood rites involving humans to sustain the Library—Meg set the rest of them to work hauling all the damaged books from the pile in the Library's atrium all the way to a back room that Meg called the book repair room.

There, Meg sorted the books into neat piles. Brigid soon found herself stitching book bindings back together with Viola while Sebastian repaired the leather covers. Beatrice fetched items and entertained the bookwyrms while Meg bustled between all of them, helping as needed and handling the worst of the books.

It was all...rather nice. Brigid fell into the rhythm of sewing, her siblings laughing and talking around her. It was far easier work than breaking their backs trying to keep their withered corn alive on their parched farm.

But she refused to be lured into letting down her guard. Even Meg seemed to have gotten complacent, but Brigid wouldn't.

"Is this what we're going to do forever?" Beatrice set the bookwyrm on the table, and it slithered between the stacks of books before curling up on a stack of random pages whose books they hadn't located yet.

"For a while, at least." Meg shrugged and gestured at the books scattered over the tables. "The Court of Knowledge is all about its Library. But I've been made the assistant librarian in charge of practical matters, like farming and such, so it doesn't have to be just about book learning. You are bound to the Court of Knowledge, so you'll be expected to earn your keep. That's only fair. But you'll be free to choose how you earn that keep. Or I suppose you can move to another Court or return to the Human Realm once you're old enough."

Meg's face fell on that last, and she looked away.

Brigid swallowed. If one of them returned to the Human Realm, they would likely be separated forever.

But what kind of future would they have here in the Fae Realm? They were human. Humans didn't belong here with the fae.

"I don't mind living here." Beatrice reached out and scratched the bookwyrm behind the ruff again. "It's fun."

"Will we learn to read?" Sebastian spread paste on the board before he stretched the leather and wrapped it tightly.

"If you want. Basil said he'd teach us." Meg paused what she was doing and glanced between them. "I know it's strange here. And it is going to be hard, living as humans among the fae in this bat-crazy realm. But it's the best thing we've got going for us since the drought hit. We're going to be fed as much food as we can eat, and we'll have a roof over our heads. And…and I know you don't know him well, yet, but Basil will be a great big brother to you."

Big brother. Brigid barely kept herself from snorting.

Did Meg really think Basil saw himself as their brother? He was their fae captor. Sure, he was putting on a good act, but Brigid couldn't let herself be fooled since Meg apparently had been.

Beatrice tugged the bookwyrm back onto her lap. It grumbled a bit but settled into place without biting her. "I like Basil. And the House. And Buddy."

"Of course you like Buddy." Viola rolled her eyes and reached for another damaged book. "But the House? The House is grumpy."

"The House is nice. It carpeted my whole room in flowers." Beatrice cuddled the bookwyrm. "Can we take this one home with us?"

"No, I think the bookwyrms need to stay in the Library, Bea." Meg smiled and reached out to pat Beatrice's knee. "But we'll be back nearly every day to work in the Library, so you'll get to see the bookwyrms then."

Brigid gritted her teeth at the beatific grin that spread across Beatrice's face. How could all of her siblings be so easily taken in? She could understand Beatrice. She was ten and easily enchanted.

But Meg? Meg had always been the sensible one. Their strong protector who had been willing to sacrifice herself to keep them safe. How could she fall for Basil's act? Especially after the stories of monsters and nearly dying that she'd briefly told them when explaining Basil's wound?

Brigid would just have to look out for all of them since Meg wouldn't, even though she had returned to them after eight months.

It turned out the stories about those snatched by the fae were true. They were never the same again, even if they came back.

Chapter Four

Brigid took up the rear again, herding her siblings through the winding pathways of the town that clustered around the castle and the Great Library. Instead of the hard packed and straight dirt roads of home, these paths were covered in either moss or short grass, winding between the homes in a willy-nilly fashion that had Brigid lost within a few minutes of leaving the House.

Most of the houses they passed were nearly identical to their House. Stone walls, thatched roof, barely bigger than their hut back home, though these houses were all likely larger on the inside. But a few of the houses were more unique, perching on stilts shaped like chicken legs or goat feet. Others were covered in scales instead, their chimneys puffing smoke as if the houses were breathing.

"The Faerie Market will be filled with many wonders and lures, and you'll be tempted more than you expect." Basil glanced over his shoulder at them, giving each of them a stern and searching look. "But whatever you do, don't touch anything unless you're prepared to bargain for it."

Brigid rolled her eyes but kept her mouth shut. Basil had gone over this several times after he and Meg had decided to take them to see the Faerie Market while it was in the Court of Knowledge.

The Faerie Market traveled between all the Courts. According to Basil, it was filled with things even the fae found inexplicable and bizarre. It did not keep to a set schedule but wandered, so a court never knew when the Market might arrive.

Unlike human markets, purchases weren't made with coins but with bargains. Sometimes the bargains would be simple things. Other times, the bargains would be dangerous and life-altering. And one could never be entirely sure which it would be until one had made the bargain, unless one was very careful and very smart about wording.

It sounded like a dangerous place to bring her siblings, but Brigid didn't have a say in it.

They turned a corner and a field spread before them, wildflowers in all colors from red to blue to deepest gold waving among the tall grass. The creek burbled along the edge of the clearing while a densely dark forest spread into the distance beyond.

Beside the creek, a caravan of brightly colored wagons had been set up with the same higgedly-piggedly rows as the town. Bright tents fluttered flags and banners among the wagons while fae of all shapes and sizes and strangeness meandered between them. The lilting notes of a wooden pipe wound around the beating of drums, the rhythms competing and clashing rather than mingling.

Basil reached out and took Meg's hand, and she smiled

up at him with that increasingly sappy look she'd been wearing around her fae husband.

The look sent a bristly feeling down Brigid's spine. What kind of enchantment was Basil using on Meg to make her go all swoony like this?

"Bea, stick close to us." Tearing herself away from Basil's smile, Meg reached behind her for Beatrice, placing a hand on her back and steering her closer to the two of them. Glancing over her shoulder, Meg gave Sebastian, Viola, and Brigid a stern look. "Try to stick close as well, but if we do get separated, make sure the three of you stick together. And remember what Basil told you."

"Yes, yes, don't touch anything. And don't even think about bargaining without asking first." Viola rolled her eyes and nudged Sebastian. "We won't forget, will we?"

"No, we won't." Sebastian nodded and gazed around the Market, as if trying to decide what to see first.

Brigid trailed along after them, feeling more alone than ever before. Viola and Sebastian had always been as thick as thieves, acting like twins even though they were a year apart. But that had never seemed to matter, since Brigid and Meg had been close.

But now a gulf had opened between her and her older sister. Meg was all enchanted with Basil now, taken in by her fae kidnapper.

As they entered the bustle of the Faerie Market, Brigid had to jump aside to avoid being run over by a tall, tree-like creature. She had to dodge again to avoid a man with horns and goat feet as he pranced through the crowd while playing a strange wooden pipe. Little green figures darted around her feet while something gray and somewhat furry scuttled behind a wagon before she got a good look at it.

A woman with a twitching mouse nose, big round ears, and a twitching pink tail held up a dress in ombre shades from deep midnight at the hem up to starry white on the bodice. "A dress for the lassie? Wear this and all your dreams will come true."

Brigid shook her head at the woman. "Even I can tell that isn't a good bargain." After all, dreams could be bad just as much as they could be good. Someone who put on that dress would very likely find themselves stuck in their worst nightmare.

"Ah, you're a canny one, I see." The mouse-woman reached under the table, fishing around for something else to tempt Brigid.

Brigid quickly looked away and hurried after her family without another word. She didn't want to risk starting a bargain by continuing the conversation.

They strolled past a booth that held what looked like birds fluttering around in gold and silver cages. When Brigid peered closer, she could see the birds were made of paper and cloth with little bits of feathers stuck onto them. The longer she looked, the more crude their appearance. Yet when she didn't look directly at them, they seemed like beautiful, song-twittering canaries.

At the next market wagon, jars of eyeballs peered and blinked at them, causing Beatrice to shriek and hide behind Meg. A row of tiny shriveled heads from some indeterminate creature dangled from the wagon's canopy. The heads twisted as if in a breeze, their eyes sewn shut. But their gaping mouths held yellowed teeth beneath ragged, withered lips. Even as Brigid watched, one of the heads turned toward her, and its gaping mouth formed the slow, rasping words, "Human child. Come closer."

Brigid shuddered and quickly stumbled back. Right into something.

Hot breath wafted over the back of her neck as a silky smooth male voice spoke with dripping disdain. "What is a human girl doing in the Faerie Market? Don't you know this place can be dangerous to your kind?"

Brigid whirled to face whoever—or whatever—she'd run into.

A tall, far too handsome fae with black hair tied back at the nape of his neck and darkly brown eyes stood too close to her. He looked to be fifteen or more years older than her, though it was hard to tell with the fae. He could be hundreds of years old for all she knew.

He brandished what was probably supposed to be a charming smile, if it wasn't so sharp-edged and dangerous. "Let me help you find your way."

She knew better than to reply to that. Instead she just glared at him and started to carefully edge away.

He reached out, as if to grab her arm, but something stopped him. A strange look crossed his face.

Before he could say anything else, Brigid turned and hurried away in the direction her family had been headed before she had been stopped.

Thankfully, she found the rest of her family had already moved on to the next booth, where an array of chocolates and candies proclaimed they would grant all sorts of things from the ability to speak to animals to the ability to fly. Not all the things were so nice. Some of the candies said they would cause flatulence or vomiting. Others would transform the victim into a rat or turn their skin and hair (or fur) purple.

Brigid wouldn't dare risk even the more benign-sounding ones. Who knew if the effects would be permanent? Or what side effects they would have on a human?

A toad creature with slimy chartreuse skin and greasy emerald hair straggling over a warty face that appeared too squashed and round to be human-like, but too angular and alive to be animal-like, wandered through the crowd pushing a cart loaded with bowls and wafting noxious smells. The toad fae croaked, "Get your skull pudding! Served chilled! Perfect for the hot summer days!"

Another shudder, and Brigid hurried on.

Basil and Meg halted next to a booth filled with a variety of glass figurines that moved and made noises. Beatrice's eyes widened at the tiny glass dog who barked a shrieking, glass woof and wagged its tail with a clinking sound as it tapped the glass trees on either side. She reached out as if to touch it but halted just short, even as Meg's hand shot out to grip her arm.

Beatrice glanced up at Basil with her big, blue eyes. "This doesn't seem so dangerous? May I have one?"

The young girl behind the table had rabbit ears and a soft cottontail. Her pink nose twitched her whiskers as she replied. "The bargain is cheap. A figurine for an answer to a question. You are a fae from the Court of Knowledge. Surely that is not such a high price."

Basil eyed the figurine for a long moment before he met the rabbit girl's eyes. "Do you give your word as a goblin that this figurine will not harm this human girl?"

"It will not harm her." The rabbit girl's nose twitched, and she pressed a slightly fur-covered hand to her chest.

"I will not give you an answer, but I will give you one fascinating fact of my choice in exchange for a figurine of her choice." Basil pointed down at Beatrice.

The rabbit girl's nose twitched even more vigorously, but then she pointed at Meg. "Not a fact of your choice, but I would like a fascinating fact about the Human Realm of her choice."

Basil glanced at Meg and met her gaze. They seemed to be speaking through a look for a long moment before Basil turned back to the goblin girl and nodded. "Very well. A fascinating fact about the Human Realm of my wife's choice in exchange for a figurine of her sister's choice."

"Done." The rabbit girl turned and blinked her long, white eyelashes at Meg expectantly.

Meg drew in a deep breath, hesitating as she stared upward as she did when thinking. Finally, she met the rabbit girl's gaze. "Where I used to live in the Human Realm, we experienced all four seasons. We had winter, spring, summer, and autumn all in one place at different times of the year."

"Really? Now that is fascinating!" The rabbit girl grinned, showing off two large front teeth. She gestured at the table. "You may take your pick."

Beatrice scrutinized the table, but she eventually reached out and picked up the little glass dog. It wagged its tail, then licked her palm.

"Ow!" Beatrice jumped and nearly dropped the dog. A tiny red line appeared on her skin.

Meg clenched her fists and glared at the rabbit girl. "You gave your word it wouldn't harm her!"

The goblin girl grinned. "It won't. That little scratch isn't deep enough to count as harm. It's glass. What else did you expect?"

Beatrice juggled the dog between her palms. "Oh. It's all

right. I'll just have to be careful." She cradled the dog between her two hands. "I think I'll call you Shimmer."

The dog made that shivering bark again and made as if to lick Beatrice's hand again. Beatrice quickly moved her thumb out of its reach before it could.

Brigid frowned. Had Basil been sweet by bargaining for the dog for Beatrice? Or was this some kind of trick? The little glass dog wasn't exactly safe.

Basil dug into the black coat he was wearing and pulled out a white handkerchief. "Here, hold it in this. That way it can't lick you."

Beatrice grinned and spread the fabric over her left hand before easing the dog back onto her now fabric-protected palm. After running in circles for another few minutes, the dog curled up on the center of her palm.

Brigid turned away, scanning the crowd of fae around them. Her skin crawled at being surrounded by so many dangerous and strange creatures. At least being bound to the Court of Knowledge had provided some protection, even if she doubted King Theseus's and Basil's motives.

She stilled, her eyes catching on a sight across the Market.

A young boy—a human boy—even younger than Sebastian was dancing wildly. His eyes were wide and scared, tears streaming down his face, even as he danced harder, as if he wasn't in control of his own body.

That black-clad fae she'd run into earlier stood behind him, arms crossed, while another hunched and craggy fae made motions with his finger as if directing the boy. The surrounding fae clapped and laughed, as if watching the poor boy getting tortured was some kind of game.

Brigid clenched her fists and started in that direction. "We have to do something."

A hand rested on her shoulder, holding her back.

When Brigid glanced over her shoulder, she found Meg there, gripping her shoulder. Meg glanced at her, then at Basil. "Basil?"

He shook his head and grimaced. "There's nothing we can do, Meg. He was snatched by Lord Chauvlyn of the Court of Revels. Even if we appealed to King Theseus, he doesn't have any authority over Lord Chauvlyn."

"But he's in the Court of Knowledge right now. Surely —" Meg glanced back at the boy.

The boy was down on all fours, eating the grass as if he was an animal. The fae around him roared with laughter.

"The Faerie Market is neutral territory while it is camped here." Basil's brows knit as he, too, stared in the direction of the human boy. "I'm sorry."

"We can't just leave him like that!" Brigid gestured at the boy. Surely this was all the proof Meg needed that Basil's kindness had just been a trick. If he was really kind, then he'd want to do something to save that poor boy.

"Robbing raccoons, Basil, look at him." Meg, too, pointed in that direction. The boy was choking and sobbing as he munched on the grass.

"I know, I know." Basil swept a hand through his hair, tousling the dark strands so that some of it fell across his forehead. He shot a look at Meg. "We'll talk about this back at the House. Let's get your siblings out of here."

Meg glanced around. Several of the fae had turned in their direction, taking them in with greedy sneers that promised that they would like nothing better than to glamour them into eating grass too. "You're right. Come on, everyone. Let's go home."

Brigid gritted her teeth and shot one last glance at the poor human boy as Basil and Meg herded them through the crowds.

Basil might not intend to rescue that poor boy, but Brigid would.

That boy had a home and a family waiting for him somewhere. Brigid knew all too well the torment of having a family member snatched by the fae and wondering what had become of them.

She couldn't let this boy's family suffer the way she had. And while Basil seemed sneaky and he must have glamoured Meg into falling in love with him, he didn't seem to have tortured her like this Lord Chauvlyn was torturing that boy. He was suffering far more than what Meg had suffered.

Somehow, someway, Brigid would rescue him and return him to his family.

Chapter Five

That night, Brigid waited until the House had gone quiet and dark. Then, she pushed aside the soft blankets and slid out of her sleeping nook. After tiptoeing across her room, she rested her hand on the Anywhere Door and eased it open. It creaked a little, but the fire in the main room remained low. A soft snuffling came from within the stable, but other than that, nothing stirred.

Brigid slipped inside, shutting the Anywhere Door behind her. Holding her breath, she crept across the space and reached the outer door.

But, when she reached for the handle, it wasn't where she expected. She paused and peered closer at the door in the dim light from the banked fire. Where was the handle? It should be right there on the door where it was earlier in the day.

Yet the planks of the wooden door remained perfectly smooth. Not a handle in sight.

Brigid grimaced and lightly banged her fist against the door. "Come on, House. Let me out."

The whole House gave a sort of shuffling around her. The door creaked, but the handle didn't appear.

"Come on. This is for a good cause." Brigid lightly kicked the door. Annoying, mostly-alive House! Why wouldn't it let her out?

The House gave another creaking shuffle around her.

With a snort, Buddy stuck his head over the stall door and blinked at her. "Brigid. What are you doing? Not trying to run away, are you?"

"No, I'm..." She wasn't sure what she should tell the talking pony companion. "I just wanted to go for a walk. I can't sleep, and I thought I'd look at the stars."

"Even I can tell that's a load of horse dung." Buddy blinked again, the look in his dark brown eyes looking less sleepy and more searching with every moment. "Tell the truth."

"I, um..." Brigid shifted, patting the door behind her. Still no handle. The House was keeping her a prisoner.

The Anywhere Door opened, and Basil stepped through, still dressed in his black coat, gray shirt, and trousers as if he had yet to go to bed.

Meg followed on his heels, also still wearing the flowing green-and-brown dress she'd been wearing earlier. "Brigid. Let me guess. You decided to go rescue that boy by yourself."

Brigid crossed her arms and glared at the two of them. "We can't just leave him! He's being tortured!"

Basil and Meg shared a look, and Basil met her gaze. "We agree."

"That's why I have to—wait, you agree?" Brigid blinked first at Basil, then at Meg.

"We've been talking about it all evening." Meg sighed and

shook her head. "You can't just storm off to steal from the Faerie Market. It doesn't quite work that way."

"We have a plan. Kind of." Basil grimaced, as if he didn't think it was a very good plan.

Meg hefted a wooden shepherd's crook. "Brigid, I'll need you to stay here with the others. Basil and I—"

"No!" Brigid couldn't let Meg go off again and leave them. It would be just like the last eight months, except this time they would be left in this strange realm without anyone to help them find their way. "You can't go. The younger ones need you. Let me go."

Basil sighed and touched Meg's cheek. "She has a point. If we were delayed, your younger siblings would be terrified to wake up here without you."

Meg rested her hand over his against her face. "I don't like the thought of you going into danger all by yourself."

"He won't be alone. He will have me." Buddy snorted, shaking his mane.

Meg half-turned and smiled at him. "Of course. How could I forget? You are a most valiant steed."

"And wise. Don't forget wise." Buddy turned his head to better eye each of them. "For something like this, you'll need an extra dose of wisdom."

"Considering this isn't a wise idea at all, I think it's a little late for that." Basil sighed and wrapped his other arm around Meg's waist, his expression sobering. "I'll feel better knowing that you're here with your family, especially with both me and Buddy away."

"*Our* family. They're your siblings too, now." Meg stood on her tiptoes and kissed his cheek. "Stay safe."

Basil turned his head and captured Meg's mouth in a deeper kiss.

Eww. Did they have to do that right in front of her? Brigid hurriedly turned away and gave the door another kick for good measure. All this could have been avoided if the House had simply let her out.

After a moment, Basil cleared his throat. "Um, well, Brigid, are you ready to go?"

"Yes." She had been ready long ago.

Meg gave her a stern look. "Listen to Basil and do whatever he tells you. You don't know the Fae Realm. It's important that you do exactly what he says, got it?"

Brigid drew in a deep breath and nodded. She would obey, as long as Basil didn't end up showing his true colors and doing something untrustworthy. If he really was going to help her rescue that boy, then she wasn't going to do anything to jeopardize it.

Buddy thunked his hoof against the stable door. "I'll meet you outside." He turned around in the stall, briefly giving them a view of his round pony flank, before he disappeared.

Brigid squared her shoulders and put her hand on the latch. This time, there was a latch, and the door swung open easily.

Frustrating, kind-of-alive House.

She stepped onto the quiet, mossy lane. The moon overhead beamed down silvery light while fireflies—or what seemed like fireflies—twinkled between the buildings and on the thatched roofs.

Basil strode out of the House behind her and closed the door with a soft click.

Brigid drew in a deep breath and faced Basil. It was the first time she had been alone with him since she and the rest of her siblings had been snatched.

What would he do, now that he had her alone? Would he keep his word and help her rescue that boy? Or would he prove he was just like all the other fae? Would he torture her?

Basil met her gaze before he cleared his throat. "Well, uh, Brigid..."

The awkward silence dragged on for a long moment as they just stared at each other, Basil shifting, Brigid with her hands on her hips.

With another hoof-thunk on the door, Buddy exited the stables. He swished his tail. "Well, are we going to do this?"

Basil nodded and strode to Buddy's side. "Lord Chauvlyn is likely still at the Market. Hopefully he is enjoying the revelry and has left the boy back at his tent."

"Enjoying the revelry?" Brigid trotted to catch up with Basil and Buddy as they set out through the quiet town.

"The Market is even wilder at night." Buddy snorted and shook his mane. "Many of the fae courts are like this all the time, especially the Court of Revels. The Court of Knowledge is a bit of an exception."

"We are about the tamest court in the entire Fae Realm, thanks to our love of knowledge over revelry and our Great Library." Basil shrugged, then grimaced, his jaw working. "Since the Faerie Market is neutral territory free of any court, it can get especially raucous and debauched at night. There's a reason I took you and your siblings there during the day."

"Oh." Brigid reached out and rested a hand on Buddy's neck as she walked. It hadn't occurred to her that the Faerie Market would be awake and even more lively at night. She had assumed she could sneak in and grab the boy while everyone slept.

The three of them walked in silence, a silence made deeper by the quiet of the town around them.

Even at night, the palace and Library on the hill above the town glowed with a greenish kind of light from within, the jewel of this fae court. Just below it, the larger estates of what Brigid assumed were the fae nobles clustered close to the palace.

As they neared the edge of town, the roar of cheering and wild laughter filled the air, along with a feral sort of music that sawed and gyrated as if intent on eating itself and all its listeners. An orange glow burned along the horizon, as if the forest were on fire.

When they rounded the final cottage, the Faerie Market flared into sight in a wild assault on the senses. Bonfires filled the field while barely dressed figures pranced around them. The colorful tents and wagons remained, but the tamer, colorful wares had been packed away. The tent of heads and eyeballs remained while even more dark and twisted items were displayed on tables and carts. Brigid tried not to look too closely at…anything. Especially not the figures tangled together in the grass with an abandon that heated her face.

When she glanced over at Basil, his face had a pink tint as well, as if he, too, found this uncomfortable.

That kind of reaction couldn't be faked. This couldn't be an act he was just putting on to lure them into a false sense of security. He truly found this as disturbing as she did.

Had she been judging him wrong this whole time?

If so, did that mean he was genuine in his care for Meg? For their siblings?

He was here, after all, helping her to steal away a stolen human boy. Surely this was a risk, even for him. Lord

Chauvlyn didn't seem the type to give up his prey easily or without a grudge.

Brigid swallowed and glanced from Buddy to Basil. "So...what's the plan?"

Buddy gave a soft snort through his big nostrils. "You were the one sneaking off. Don't you have a plan?"

She really should have thought this through better than she had. She winced. "Um, no?"

Basil sighed and swung his gaze back to the Faerie Market. "Buddy, can you scout the Market? Find the boy and make sure Lord Chauvlyn isn't with him. You're a talking equine companion. The revelers won't pay any attention to you."

Buddy bobbed his head. "Wise decision. Stay here."

With a twitch of his tail, Buddy trotted off across the field.

The fae dancing around the fires and clustered around the booths selling a drink that seemed to make the fae even more deliriously wild than before didn't even glance at Buddy.

Was there some kind of prejudice against talking equine companions? Were they almost considered a servant by the other fae? That would make sense. Servants and peasants were always invisible. Hopefully that meant Basil was right and Buddy wouldn't attract attention.

Within moments, Buddy disappeared among the tents and revelry.

Basil knelt next to a tree, using it for shelter to stay out of sight of the Market. "We might as well get comfortable while we wait."

Brigid eased to the mossy ground, glad when it wasn't as damp as she'd feared. Hopefully the ground wouldn't stain her dress, another lovely thing of pink silk and trimmed in lace.

What was she supposed to say to Basil while they waited? This seemed like the moment for some kind of bonding discussion.

If Basil was truly the sincere and sweet master librarian that he appeared to be, then he wasn't Meg's fae captor. He really was her husband, as both she and Basil had claimed. They really loved each other.

And that would make him really Brigid's brother-in-law, the first big brother she'd ever had.

The truth was right there, staring her in the face the whole time. Despite all of her warnings and worries, it turned out Meg had been right all along. Basil was exactly who he seemed. Brigid could no longer deny it, especially when he was here, being very big brother-ish, by helping her rescue the human boy.

"The eight months while Meg was gone must have been hard." Basil glanced over his shoulder, then leaned against the tree.

"They were." Brigid didn't want to talk about those months of trying to come up with whatever lie she could to put Cullen off as long as possible. "So...Meg..."

Basil shifted and tugged at his collar. "I love your sister, if that's what you were going to ask."

"Yes, but I guess that answer was obvious." Brigid forced herself to grin. It had been obvious, even if she hadn't wanted to see it before now. "So you didn't actually snatch her?"

"I did, kind of." Basil shifted again, looking down at the moss instead of at her. "Buddy talked me into going to the Human Realm. I didn't think I'd actually snatch a bride. But then Meg was there and she seemed to want to be taken. And one thing led to another and, well, your sister is amazing. I wouldn't have survived Midsummer Night without her. She pushes me to look beyond myself and the Library in a way I never have before."

Brigid swallowed and couldn't meet Basil's gaze. He was far too sincere and honest. Strange, for a fae. Especially a fae here in his own realm where he could lie freely. It was only in the Human Realm where he would be restricted from lying. Except hadn't Meg mentioned that he was free of that restriction thanks to his marriage to a human? "Meg seems happy here."

"I hope she is." Basil gave another little shrug. "I hope all of you will be."

Brigid found herself giving Basil a tentative smile. "I think we might. I know Beatrice is already happy. Sebastian probably will be utterly happy once he gets his first sword lesson, and I think Viola is already falling in love with the Great Library."

"And you?" Basil's voice went as soft as his brown eyes. Caring in a way she hadn't expected from the fae she had assumed was her sister's kidnapper.

"I don't know." Brigid drew up her knees and rested her chin on them. Her younger siblings could easily adapt to a new life in a new realm. They were young enough that they might have time to have dreams about their future.

But Brigid had given up on dreams long ago. Sometime between her parents dying, Meg disappearing, and Cullen's threats, she had lost the ability to innocently dream about a future for herself. It was best not to think about the future when it likely consisted of slavery and an early death.

What would she do in the Fae Realm? The Great Library

seemed nice, but she wasn't sure she wanted to spend her days in the book repair room with Meg, fixing books, cuddling bookwyrms, and talking to the sentient Library.

Basil drew in a breath, though he paused as if he didn't know what to say.

Before he had to come up with a reply, the clopping of hooves approached them.

Brigid peeked around the tree, breathing out a sigh of relief when she saw Buddy trotting back toward them.

None of them spoke until Buddy joined them inside the tree line, sheltered by the large trees and the tangled vines from the sight of those cavorting around the bonfires.

Buddy leaned his head closer to them. "Lord Chauvlyn is by those drinking faerie wine, but he doesn't seem to be drinking himself. The boy is tied to a stake by Lord Chauvlyn's tent. It appears the poor thing collapsed in exhaustion."

Brigid clenched her fists until her knuckles whitened. They simply had to get the boy out of here.

Basil pushed to his feet. "Let's go rescue him."

Brigid drew in a deep breath. It was her turn to come up with the plan. "Actually, it would probably be best if Buddy and I went to rescue the boy. He might be scared to be taken off by another fae. Could you keep an eye on Lord Chauvlyn and alert us if he starts heading back to his tent?"

"I could do that." Basil straightened his coat, then hesitated. He pulled off his coat and held it out to Brigid. "Take this. It is too distinct. I'd rather not look like a librarian at the party."

Brigid took the coat. Then, after hesitating, she shrugged into it. It was far too big at the shoulders and arms, but it was still warm and smelled faintly of the same scent as one of the bottles of soaps in the bathing grotto. The black color would make sneaking easier.

Basil ruffled his own hair, then unbuttoned his shirt nearly to his naval. To complete the look, he rolled his sleeves up, but in a rough, haphazard fashion.

Buddy bobbed his head again. "Better slop some faerie wine on yourself to complete the look."

Basil grimaced but nodded. "I'll meet the two of you back here." With one last look in their direction, Basil headed for the Market. As he neared the revelry, he added a languid stagger to his walk.

Brigid swallowed and rested her hand on Buddy's shoulder. She kept her head down behind Buddy's neck as they stuck to the shadows and circled around the Market.

Buddy slowed, tiptoeing as much as a pony could. He led Brigid toward a cluster of tents at the edge of the Market. There, a smaller campfire lit the front of a black tent flying a dark green flag. One of those talking skulls hung from the front of the tent.

A wooden stake had been driven into the ground. It had a metal ring bolted to the top while a small length of chain connected it to a metal collar around the poor human boy's neck.

The sight turned Brigid's stomach. She had been so very wrong about Basil. Instead of chains and torture, he had given them clothes and a home.

But this boy was suffering the torments of the fae.

She started forward, but Buddy's teeth snapped onto the back of her dress and dragged her back. She glanced over her shoulder at him. "What?"

Buddy released her and pointed his nose in the direction of the tent. "That head is going to shriek loud enough to drag a banshee from the Realm of Monsters if we cross into Lord Chauvlyn's camp."

"Oh." She hadn't anticipated that. She should have, though. Of course Lord Chauvlyn wouldn't make it easy. "How do we sneak in there, then? Is there any way to fool one of those heads?"

Buddy shook his head. "Any fae or human who gets too close will set it off."

That was a problem.

They couldn't go in there, but...

Brigid gestured at the forest behind them. "What about a branch? Or a tree? Would that set it off?"

Buddy tilted his head, then shook his head. "No, that shouldn't set it off."

Brigid grinned. "Then I have an idea. The Market is neutral territory, but this surrounding forest is still the territory of the Court of Knowledge, correct?"

"Yes." Buddy nudged her with his nose. "I like you. You're clever, when you stop and think."

"Thanks." Brigid crept deeper into the trees until she found a sapling about the right size. She gripped it and drew in a deep breath. She hoped this worked like it was supposed to. This forest was kind of alive, like everything else seemed to be in the Fae Realm. "I need to borrow you for a few minutes. I'll put you right back after I'm done."

She held her breath, waiting and trying to send all her feelings of desperation and the rightness of her cause into the tree.

After several heartbeats, the dirt around the base of the tree rippled. The roots pulled from the ground, and the sapling sagged into her hand.

"Thank you." Brigid carried the tree back to where Buddy still stood. "Wait here."

She crouched and sneaked closer to the camp. When she was about five feet away, the head swung toward her, its mouth gaping as if in preparation to scream.

Brigid eased back a step, and the head swung away again. Good. Now she knew where the boundary was.

She dropped to her stomach and eased the sapling forward. The head remained where it was, swaying slightly in the evening breeze.

Carefully, she reached with the branch until she nudged the head's string with the top branch. She tightened her grip on the sapling, trying to convey what she wanted.

After a moment, the sapling wrapped its top branch around the string.

"Good tree." Brigid gave a sharp tug backwards. The head came free, swinging from the end of her sapling. She willed the sapling to understand what she wanted, then she flicked the sapling as she might have a stick fishing pole.

The head swung, then the sapling let it go at the right moment. The head sailed a few yards farther away, landing in another empty camp before a red tent.

There, they were safe to enter.

First, Brigid pushed to her feet, then jogged back to the forest. She located the disturbed dirt and set the tree back on the ground.

It gave a little happy shiver as it wove its roots back into the ground.

"Thank you. You may have helped save a life tonight." Brigid patted its trunk, then headed back to Buddy's side.

How much time did they have left? Would Lord

Chauvlyn return to check on his human captive sooner rather than later?

The human boy still lay on the ground, curled with his knees to his chest and his arms over his head even in his sleep.

Brigid held her breath as she knelt at the boy's side, but the head didn't start shrieking. She inspected the chain. How were they going to free the boy? Lord Chauvlyn likely had the key on him, and this was faerie steel. Even a blacksmith back home wouldn't be able to break it.

They would have to figure it out later, after they sneaked the boy out of here.

Brigid rested a hand on the boy's shoulder and shook him. He mumbled but didn't fully wake.

She shook him again, harder.

The boy bolted upright and threw himself backward in a jangle of chains, his eyes huge. "Who…who are you?"

"I'm a friend." Brigid held out one hand, palm up. With the other, she brushed back her hair to show the boy her rounded, human ear. "I'm a human. I just came through the faerie circle a few days ago. I'm going to get you out of here and get you home."

The frightened look in the boy's eyes faded, and his shoulders relaxed. "Thank you."

This boy could have been Sebastian. How easily the fae could have snatched one of Brigid's siblings instead of this boy.

Other places in the kingdom, like the southern Greenwood, had their foresters who protected the people from fae. But the rural farming villages didn't. They were too poor for the king to even worry if a few villagers went missing.

Brigid gripped the stake and tried to wiggle it. It was stuck fast into the ground and barely moved. She faced the boy again. "I'm going to ask my talking pony companion to come over here, all right? Don't scream."

When the boy nodded, Brigid waved to Buddy.

Buddy trotted over. The boy cowered at the end of his chain, leaning toward Brigid. But he didn't scream.

After sniffing the wooden stake, Buddy turned around, cocked a rear hoof, and gave the stake a solid kick.

The top of the stake snapped off with a sharp crack.

Brigid grabbed the chain. "Let's go. We can figure out how to get you out of this once we are away from here."

The boy nodded, then stumbled to his feet. He managed two staggering steps, his face whitening.

This wasn't going to work. The poor boy had been tortured within an inch of utter exhaustion. Of course he wasn't up for late night escapes.

Buddy glanced back, then halted and knelt to lower his back.

Brigid approached the boy cautiously. "May I help you on?"

After a moment, the boy nodded and crept closer to Buddy. He flinched when Brigid gripped his waist, but he didn't cry out or pull away. Brigid boosted him onto Buddy's back, where the boy hunched and gripped Buddy's mane hard enough that it was likely painful. But Buddy didn't reprimand the boy.

Brigid hurried at Buddy's side, still gripping the end of the chain. She held her breath as they trotted away from the tents, the raucous laughter of the gallivanting fae fading the farther they disappeared into the forest.

Still, she didn't dare relax until they had the boy safely home in the Human Realm.

She and Buddy halted a few yards into the tree line near where they had parted from Basil earlier. Where was her brother-in-law? Shouldn't he have been here already?

Perhaps they should have worked out a better system to alert each other. Or a time to meet back here. Come to think of it, they really should have gone into this with an actual plan.

"How long should we wait here for Basil?" Brigid leaned closer to Buddy, glancing back toward the Market.

"Basil?" The boy hunched lower over Buddy's neck.

"My brother-in-law." Brigid swallowed and forced herself to meet the boy's gaze with more confidence than she felt. "He's fae, but he's one of the good ones, I think. He married my sister and rescued our whole family from a bad situation back in the Human Realm."

"He's the best." Buddy swished his tail, ducking his head so that Brigid couldn't see the expression on his fuzzy, pony face.

But there was a roughness to his voice that wasn't usually there.

Brigid remembered how Buddy had gone into the Market, expecting to be invisible to the partying fae. Yet Basil always treated Buddy as a friend or one of the family. To Basil, Buddy wasn't a servant. He was truly a companion.

Loud crunching approached through the forest.

Buddy shifted, keeping the boy hidden behind a large tree. Brigid tucked closer to Buddy. If that was Lord Chauvlyn, she would tell Buddy to run with the boy. She was bound to the Court of Knowledge. Hopefully that would protect her. But the boy wouldn't be safe.

A figure staggered into view between the trees. He lifted his head, smiled, and gave a little wave.

Basil. But he still tottered even as he reached them, grinning in a lazy, vague way that Brigid had yet to see from him. He reeked of something sickly sweet that sent a buzzing into Brigid's head. He all but fell against Buddy, wrapping an arm around the pony's neck.

Brigid reached out, though she halted before steadying her brother-in-law. "Are you all right?"

"Just the smell of the faerie fruit is making me a bit woozy." Basil grimaced and sucked in a deep breath. "Don't know how the other fae can stand the stuff."

"Do you need to climb onto my back too?" Buddy nipped at the tail of Basil's shirt.

"I'm fine." Basil pushed off Buddy to straighten a bit. "Let's get moving. Lord Chauvlyn didn't look like he planned to observe the revelries much longer."

Brigid couldn't stop a shiver. She didn't want to be caught by Lord Chauvlyn once he realized they had stolen his captive.

The boy hunched further on Buddy's back, his eyes wide as he stared at Basil as if he expected him to start tormenting him at any moment.

Together, they set out into the forest once again. The farther they walked, surrounded by the crisp, damp smell of the nighttime forest laced with the sweet thickness of the fae air, the steadier Basil became, as if the effects of the faerie fruit were wearing off.

If faerie fruit had this much effect on the fae, the legends of what the fruit did to humans weren't exaggerated. According to the stories, just a bite of faerie fruit could put a human entirely in the power of the fae. Humans could become addicted, living in a hazy state while the fae toyed with them as they pleased. If they ate enough faerie fruit, they would die if they tried to leave the Fae Realm.

Brigid glanced up at the boy huddled on Buddy's back. "You didn't eat any faerie fruit while you were here, did you?"

The boy grimaced. "I had some. Today. That's how he made me eat the grass. But I ain't a fool. I know the stories. I ate as little as possible."

Brigid gritted her teeth. And she had thought Cullen was evil.

At least the boy didn't seem addicted to faerie fruit. That was something. Even if it sounded like the poor boy would have a lot of trauma to work through.

Had she truly managed to save him? Or would what he had experienced haunt him for his entire life?

There was nothing more she could do for him but help him get back to the Human Realm and hope he managed to recover enough to live a good life.

A scattering of the small red flowers carpeted the forest floor a moment before they reached the circle of trees and stones that marked the faerie circle.

"Hold on tight, everyone," Buddy stated, a moment before he stepped into the circle.

Brigid kept one hand on the boy's back and the other wrapped in Buddy's mane as that same upside-down feeling squeezed around her. Her breath caught in her chest, but this time she didn't fight the feeling. She let herself fall into the swirling, catching glimpses of people and places and times that made no sense though they almost felt like they should.

Then Buddy took another step, and she gasped in a

breath of air that was dry, dusty, and strangely thin compared to the thick, floral air of the Fae Realm.

Spindly, parched trees surrounded them while the dirt where they stood, just outside of the faerie circle, was dry and dead. And familiar. It was the same fae circle where she and her family had left the Human Realm only a few days ago. Or was it years ago here in the Human Realm? She didn't know.

Brigid turned to the boy on Buddy's back. "This is a stand of forest outside of the town of Burgwood where I used to live. Can you find your way home from here? Or do you need us to go with you?"

The boy glanced at them, his gaze focusing on Basil the longest, then shook his head. "No, I can get home from here. I'm from the next town over."

As much as it was nice to return home, Brigid didn't want to stay longer than she had to. Her siblings were back in the Fae Realm, and it was time she figured out how to make a new life for herself there.

"All right." She gestured at the chain. "I'm sorry we couldn't help you with that."

The boy shrugged. "I'll be able to pick the lock now that I'll have time without Lord Chauvlyn noticing. I bet I can get a good price for a bit of faerie steel at the village."

The longer he spoke, the more the slump to his shoulders faded, the brightness in his eyes returning. As if he was beginning to truly believe that he was free.

Buddy knelt, and the boy slid off his back. The boy took two steps in the direction of town before he turned around and faced them again. "Thanks. You didn't have to do this, and I didn't think I'd ever...just thanks."

"It was the right thing to do." Brigid gave the boy a smile

and a little wave. It seemed wrong, to just dump him off in the forest without helping him all the way home. But they had done all they could for him. It was up to him from here. "I hope you get home all right."

How long would it have been in the Human Realm since this boy had been snatched? Would he even have a home to return to? Due to the drought, many people had been sold into indentured servitude and few people would be willing to take in a boy alone if his family was dead or gone.

But what else could she do? She had rescued him from the torments of the Fae Realm. It would have to be enough.

The boy nodded, turned, then trudged away into the forest. She, Buddy, and Basil remained where they were, watching him leave, until he disappeared into the dry, dark night.

Chapter Six

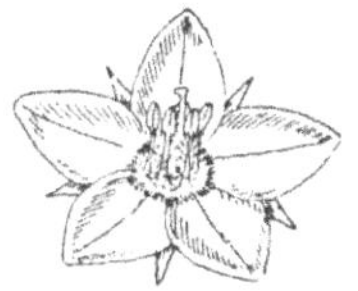

Brigid gasped as she stepped back into the Fae Realm. It was still night, and she hoped that meant that it was still the same night they'd left.

Basil patted Buddy's neck. "Let's go home. I'm sure Meg is getting worried."

Brigid fell into step beside her brother-in-law and his talking pony companion. She should thank them for their help. But when she opened her mouth, all that came out was, "What kind of flowers are these?" She pointed at the red flowers decorating the moss below their feet.

"They are the wild fae primrose. They originally came from the Human Realm. I think they might be called pimpernel or something like that in your world." Basil reached down, plucked one, then held it out to her. "They tend to grow in and around faerie circles, and the stories say they lead wanderers home."

Brigid took the flower, turning its stem in her fingers. Had these flowers led her home? The Fae Realm didn't yet feel like home, not really.

But what was home but family, and her family was here. This realm would be her home, and the rest of her family was quickly becoming happy here. She would just have to find a way to be happy too.

Brigid glanced at Basil, then the flower she still gripped in her hand, then back at Basil. She drew in a deep breath. She had to get this out before they returned to the House. "Thank you. Both of you. I wouldn't have been able to rescue that boy without your help."

"It was the right thing to do." Basil shrugged and rubbed at the back of his neck, not looking at her as if he found her thanks embarrassing. "We're just lucky that Puck hasn't returned from the Human Realm yet. He would have made it much harder to sneak around the Market. He always tends to turn up when you aren't looking."

Brigid swallowed and nodded. This could have gone much worse. They probably shouldn't have gotten away with this, given how little of a plan they'd had.

She drew in a deep breath. She had to get these words out. "I think I needed a big brother after all."

Basil skidded to a halt, gaping at her for a moment. Then, a broad smile crossed his angular fae face, the too-handsomeness tempered by his air of adorable awkwardness. "I always wanted siblings."

"Well, now you have four of them." Brigid grinned back.

It was almost surreal to enter the quiet fae village, stroll down the mossy lanes that were becoming more familiar every day, and open the door to the little stone cottage with a thatched roof.

As they entered, the House trembled, as if releasing a huffy, relieved breath.

Inside, Meg jumped to her feet. "Blistering badgers,

you're both all right!" She raced across the room and threw herself into Basil's arms.

Her brother-in-law caught Meg and wrapped his arms around her, holding her close.

Brigid glanced away before they started kissing.

Buddy stuck his head over the half door to the stable. "I'm all right too, in case anyone wants to know. Thanks for asking."

Brigid crossed the room and patted his nose. "Meg was right. You are a valiant steed. We wouldn't have been able to do any of this without you."

Buddy flicked his ears, a horse grin crossing his face.

Meg and Basil stepped apart, and Meg smoothed her hands over Basil's rumbled shirt, her gaze dropping to the view of his chest thanks to his shirt's unbuttoned state. "You look rather good all disheveled. What happened?"

"Long story." Basil plucked at a damp spot on his shirt.

Oh, right. Brigid was still wearing her brother-in-law's librarian coat. It had been rather nice and warm while they had been trudging back through the forest. She shrugged out of the coat and held it out to Basil. "Uh, here. Thanks for letting me wear it tonight."

He grinned and took the coat. "Thanks for looking after it for me."

When their gazes met, Brigid finally felt it. The feeling of home wrapping around her like the warm, soft blankets waiting for her in her sleeping nook. She wasn't sure what this new life here would look like, but this place would be home, one way or another.

"Now that you're all back safe, let's get back to bed. We might be able to catch a little bit of sleep before our morning shift at the Library." Meg wrapped her arm around

Basil's waist, giving him a little tug toward the Anywhere Door. The way her gaze was warm and focused on Basil had Brigid wishing she was anywhere but in the room with them. They didn't look like they wanted her there either at that particular moment.

Brigid made a break for the Anywhere Door and beat her sister and brother-in-law to it. She all but dove through the Anywhere Door, thankful when the House didn't play any tricks on her and she actually ended up in her room.

She fell into the sleeping nook in the clothes she was wearing since they were comfortable enough. The last thing she did before rolling into her blankets to fall asleep was stick the red primrose into the moss.

BRIGID WOKE with a start as the House tossed her out of her bed nook without any warning. She hit the floor in a tangle of blankets, her face pressed into the green-tasting moss.

Spitting, she rolled into a sitting position and rubbed first at her eyes, then at her side where she'd hit the floor. It hadn't hurt, not really. The moss helped soften the landing.

"What was that for?" She glared up at the ceiling.

The House gave a shudder around her, shaking a bit of dirt onto her head.

"Fine, fine. I'm up." Brigid pushed to her feet, halting as she caught sight of a cluster of three tiny red flowers growing from the moss next to her sleeping nook. There had been only the one blossom when she'd stuck it there last night. Had it somehow planted itself in the moss? And was now growing there?

Whatever had happened, the sight made her smile. Another reminder that this was home.

As soon as she set the blanket on the bed, the moss beneath her feet rolled. She staggered across the room and tripped into the Anywhere Door. It opened before she could even process where she wanted to go.

She tumbled into the main room of the cottage, barely catching herself before she fell flat on her face.

Basil and Meg were already there, with Buddy looking in over the stable door.

At the doorway, a thin, blond-haired fae man stood in the room, facing Basil and Meg.

Meg turned to Brigid with a tight look. "Brigid, please stay here with the others. Basil and I have been summoned to meet with King Theseus and Queen Hippolyta."

This was about last night. Meg hadn't said it out loud, but the way she, Basil, and Buddy were exchanging looks, they all suspected it was the case.

"I should go too." Brigid met Meg's gaze. "If this is about...well, I can't let you and Basil take all the blame."

The fae turned to Brigid and raised his eyebrows. "Blame for what, miss?"

"I'm not saying anything more. I just think I should go." Brigid crossed her arms.

Basil rested a hand on Meg's shoulder, holding her gaze for a moment before he nodded to Brigid. "All right, you can come. But let us do the talking. Buddy, stay here."

Buddy bobbed his head and gave a low snort. "I will look after them. I'm sure you'll be back shortly."

Basil turned to the fae waiting just inside the door with an expression that seemed to ask if that would be the case.

The fae's expression didn't flicker from its blank, professional one. Nothing to give away what he thought about their chances of returning home before the others woke up. Instead, he gestured toward the Anywhere Door. "Could we use your Anywhere Door to travel to the palace?"

Basil nodded, then led the way. Meg rested a hand on Brigid's back and steered her toward the door. The fae followed them, a looming presence at their backs.

When Basil opened the door, it led to the white marble hall of Anywhere Doors. After stepping through and closing the door behind them, the fae led them to the left, toward the double doors on the far end that led to the palace instead of the Great Library on the other.

The swordmaidens guarding the doors nodded to the fae and let them stroll by. Inside, Brigid found herself in an entry hall of marble with deep green runners down the halls and up the broad, marble stairs. Portraits hung on the walls, their frames made of winding branches and sprouting flowers. The statues on the pedestals on either side of the hall moved and giggled or paged through marble books as if searching for a particular obscure piece of knowledge.

The fae continued leading them briskly down the hall before he turned left into a room. Huge windows overlooked the town below while the upper parts of the windows were formed of stained glass depicting trees and flowers.

But she couldn't concentrate on the plush decorations.

Lord Chauvlyn stood in front of the large, dark wood desk that was strewn with books and papers. Behind the desk, King Theseus had his arms crossed while Queen Hippolyta stood at his side, clinking in her chain mail and resting her hand on her sword as if she'd dearly love to draw it.

No love lost there. Hopefully that was a good thing for Brigid and her family.

The fae who had led them here bowed. "Your Majesties, announcing Master Librarian Basil, Assistant Librarian Margaret, and Apprentice Librarian Brigid, as you requested."

"Thank you, Philostrate." King Theseus nodded to the fae.

Philostrate bowed again, then took a place next to the door.

Lord Chauvlyn's dark eyes swept over them, lingering on Brigid, before he turned back to King Theseus. "I demand to be compensated for the human that was stolen from me."

Brigid sucked in a breath, but Meg's hand clamped onto her arm. Meg shot her a glare. A warning to stay silent.

King Theseus met Lord Chauvlyn glare for glare. "You marched into my palace and have been making demands, yet you have no proof any member of my Court was involved."

Lord Chauvlyn snorted and gestured at them. "You know the laws. My property was stolen while on neutral territory. No fae would dare break the laws of the Market like that. Only a human would. And you happen to have a family of humans residing in your Court. I saw them in the Market earlier in the day."

Basil drew his shoulders straight, his face nearly as blank as Philostrate's had been. "I was showing my wife and her family the Faerie Market for the first time. We went to the Market, bargained for a few things for her family, then went home."

Queen Hippolyta sidled a step closer to Lord Chauvlyn.

"The Market might be neutral territory, but if your property was rightfully stolen and the person got away with it, then I don't see the problem here. By our laws, the human has been stolen away again, and you have no recourse except to steal the human back if you so wish. The laws of hospitality aren't as binding as the Laws of Bindings, after all." She turned to Basil. "Do you have Lord Chauvlyn's human boy hiding in your cottage?"

"No." Basil held the queen's gaze without flinching. "The only humans in my cottage are Meg's family."

Lord Chauvlyn scowled and waved at Basil. "That does not mean much. We are not in the Human Realm. He can lie as easily as any human."

"Perhaps. But it is very hard for fae to lie to their monarchs." Queen Hippolyta eyed Lord Chauvlyn with a gaze that was as steely as her sword. "And I am Basil's queen."

"You heard my queen and my librarian. Basil doesn't have anything that belongs to you." King Theseus held out his hands in a way that somehow brooked no argument and yet was placating at the same time. "I'm sorry the hospitality of the Market was broken, but from what I can see, the boy was snatched and is no longer yours. Now, I don't believe I owe you anything. Return to the Market or return to your Court, but leave my librarians alone."

For a moment, Lord Chauvlyn's jaw worked. Then he clicked his heels together, bowed, and marched toward the door.

As he passed Basil, Meg, and Brigid, Lord Chauvlyn halted and gave each of them one last, piercing look. Then, he swept out of the room, Philostrate falling in at his heels.

After the door closed, all of them remained silent for

another few minutes, as if to ensure Lord Chauvlyn was truly gone.

Then, King Theseus slumped into the chair behind his desk. "Tell me the truth, Master Librarian Basil. Did you steal that human boy away?"

Brigid quickly stepped forward before Basil or Meg could take the blame for this. "No, I did."

Basil hurried to step in front of her. "The fault is mine. Brigid doesn't know our ways. I was the one who should take the blame. I knowingly helped her. I'm the one who broke the laws of the Market."

Brigid shoved under her brother-in-law's arm. "I'm the one who actually stole the boy from Lord Chauvlyn's campsite. All Basil did was keep watch and walk along with me. But I'm the one who did the actual stealing. I'm the one who wanted to rescue the boy, and Basil just came along to make sure I was safe. I talked him into it." Brigid planted herself in front of Basil and she nudged him with her elbow when he made a noise as if to interrupt her. Instead, she met King Theseus's gaze without flinching. "And I would do it all over again. What Lord Chauvlyn was doing was cruel. Humans are people too. They shouldn't be treated like slaves to be tormented for entertainment. It's a disgusting practice, and I couldn't stand by while that boy was being held captive."

Queen Hippolyta gracefully perched on the corner of the desk, sweeping aside a few books to make room. "I'm glad to hear it."

"I—you are?" Brigid gaped at the fae queen.

"Yes. I quite agree that the practice of stealing humans for sport is disgusting." Queen Hippolyta languidly leaned her hand on Theseus's desk. With her other hand, she reached back, glancing at her husband.

King Theseus clasped her hand, giving her a returning smile, before he turned back to them. "Hippolyta and I wish to make our Courts a haven for the peaceable and down-trodden among the Fae Realm. Hippolyta's Court of Swordmaidens protects women. My Court protects families and everyone else seeking knowledge and sanctuary."

Hippolyta squeezed Theseus's hand and took over as if finishing his thought for him. "We have become more aware of the plight of humans in the Fae Realm. There are those like Meg who are cherished and find true homes here. But many others—far too many—are snatched by those like Lord Chauvlyn. It is wrong, and we would like to help."

They would? For the first time that morning, Brigid felt like she could breathe. Perhaps she hadn't messed up every-thing for her family in their new home.

"But it's complicated." Theseus sighed. "If we started actively stealing humans back from the other Courts, it would bring down their wrath on the Court of Knowledge. Even the might of the Court of Swordmaidens wouldn't be enough to protect us. It would jeopardize the Library and all those to whom we have already given shelter."

"But you may have provided us with the answer, Brigid." Hippolyta smiled, an expression that held both warmth and a sharpness that sent a shiver down Brigid's spine. Hippolyta glanced over her shoulder at Theseus once again. "Theseus, mine, I fear I'll need to snatch one of the members of your Court away from you."

"Oh, really. What will I gain in return?" Theseus lifted the hand he still held and kissed her knuckles.

Hippolyta sent him a grin both coy and a touch savage. "The safety that if this goes wrong, the blame will fall on my

Court rather than yours. And, perhaps, we can discuss the terms after dinner tonight."

"As you wish, my lady." Theseus kissed her hand again, lingering a bit longer.

Brigid shifted and looked away. Was it really appropriate for them to be watching while their king and queen looked at each other like that?

At least it was a little better than when Basil and Meg gave each other those eyes.

Meg joined Brigid and rested a hand on her shoulder. "What do you want Brigid to do? She's only sixteen. She's too young to be involved in snatching humans or anything like that."

"Well, she pulled it off well enough last night, it seems." Hippolyta's mouth twitched, as if she was impressed in spite of herself. "But, I agree that she will need training before she takes this on."

"*If* she takes this on. Snatching humans would be dangerous." Basil stepped up to her other side, a solid, big brother presence as if he intended to stand up to his king and queen to protect her.

Brigid drew her shoulders straight and let her gaze drift to the stained glass windows. Tiny, five-petaled red flowers wound through the borders of the windows. The wild fae primrose, calling wanderers home.

She hadn't known what the purpose of her life would be. But here in the Fae Realm, perhaps she'd found it. She would make sure no family had to suffer as she had during those eight months when Meg had been missing.

"I'll do it." Brigid crossed her arms and faced King Theseus and Queen Hippolyta. "What do you want me to do?"

"We want you to take on the job of returning humans to their realm." Theseus's voice dropped. "Once you take on this role, we won't be able to help you. At least, not officially. You'll be mostly on your own."

"I will provide training, of course." Hippolyta tapped her sword's hilt. "I will not send you into this unprepared. You are young. I fear you will have to be patient and take the time to learn and grow before you take on your first mission."

Brigid nodded. If last night had taught her anything, it was how unprepared she was. She needed to take the time to learn. Not just how to fight or whatever Queen Hippolyta wanted to teach her, but also about the fae, their laws, and their Courts. She had so blindly stumbled around last night. She could have gotten herself, Buddy, and Basil hurt. She had risked the safety of her entire family.

As much as she hurt for the humans currently in the clutches of the fae, she could not save them. Not right now, anyway. It would do no one any good if she were caught on her first—well, second—attempt. If she learned and had the skills to be smart about this, she could save many, many lives.

Hippolyta glided to her feet and sidled toward Brigid. "By the time you're finished training, you will have the skills to get yourself in and out of danger. But it will be up to you whether you have the smarts to pull this off. You will need to out-fae the fae to protect yourself and those you love. You cannot let even a whiff of suspicion fall on yourself. Otherwise, you will put your siblings and your Court in danger. Do you understand?"

Brigid met the queen's hard eyes and nodded. "I will not let you down."

And she wouldn't. She hadn't been able to help Meg, though it turned out Meg had been safe all along. She hadn't been able to protect her siblings from Cullen. Meg and Basil had done that, in the end.

But Brigid could do this. She could save all those humans who weren't snatched by someone like Basil. Who had found only torments instead of a home in the Fae Realm.

She would become the Wild Fae Primrose, leading wanderers home.

After Robin Hood

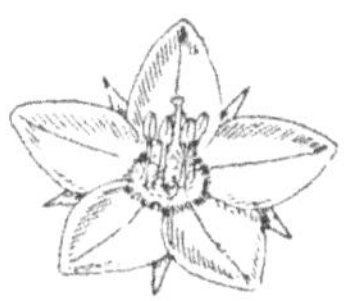

Munch leaned against a tree as the sun set, the beams of sunlight bathing the castle walls before him and highlighting the flapping piece of white cloth hanging out of a window on the fourth floor of the nearest tower. Any moment now, Robin would take down that cloth, signaling that she had survived another day in the home of the murderous Duke Guy "Bluebeard" of Gysborn.

The duke had just arrived home a few minutes ago. Watching the duke's traveling party exit the forest and enter the castle had been the only interesting thing during Munch's entire shift on castle watch. Well, there was that squirrel that kept racing up and down a nearby tree. But that was it.

Who knew that having his sister marry a murdering duke would turn out to be so boring? Especially for Munch. As the youngest of five brothers and one rather reckless sister, he wasn't trusted with a lot of the planning. Or the more interesting parts of the plan.

No, it was all, *Watch the castle, Munch. Don't fall asleep on watch, Munch. Don't eat all the food while we're gone, Munch.*

His siblings still saw him as the little boy he'd been when their parents had been killed. Not the eighteen-year-old adult that he was now.

Munch dug into his pocket and pulled out the chunk of bread he'd stuffed in there earlier in the day. His older brothers mocked him for always eating, but why wouldn't he? He had five older brothers and an older sister who was just as bad when it came to mealtimes. He had to pinch food where he could if he wanted to eat.

As he lifted the bread to his mouth, the white cloth left the window. But instead of being taken inside as before, this time it fluttered down the side of the castle.

Munch straightened, squinting through the gathering gloom of dusk at the tower. Was that Robin, partially out the window? He only caught a glimpse of her before she disappeared back inside.

He shoved the bread back into his pocket before he jumped to his feet. Something was wrong. Robin was in trouble.

Munch fumbled for the horn at his waist. Over his family's years of haunting the Greenwood as outlaws, they had used the signal horns rarely, since the sound would carry and give away their location to the duke and his men. But the horns were an old, forester tradition, used to signal where fae or their monsters had stepped through the faerie circles into the Greenwood.

Now was the time to use this horn.

Munch ripped it from its ties and brought it to his mouth. For a moment, his chest was squeezing too tightly, his hands shaking too much.

Robin needed him. *Him.* The youngest brother who never did anything heroic and was never trusted with the key parts of the plans. Even when he thought he'd play a role—as Robin's guard—he'd ended up being sent away back to the forest.

This time, everything was up to him.

Munch dragged in a breath, put his mouth to the horn, and blew out a long, ringing note that carried through the nighttime forest.

He paced while he waited, the darkness gathering around him. Even as he waited, fae magic flared around the castle, so strong that even Munch could taste its overpowering sickly sweet and floral taste in the back of his mouth.

With a crunching of leaves, Will raced out of the forest, his quiver on his back and his bow already strung. John and Tuck were hot on his heels, their jaws tight, with Alan and Marion hurrying behind them.

Munch pointed toward the castle. "She tossed the white cloth out the window. It looked like she was trying to go out the window before she was yanked back, but I couldn't get a good look."

Will's jaw tightened, his brown eyes flinty. "Then let's get her out of there."

Munch swallowed and fell in at the rear of his pack of brothers. Robin so rarely needed them to bail her out. Sure, she got in a few scrapes, but she always wiggled her way out of them just as flamboyantly.

Will raced toward the castle in the lead, though his steps slowed as he neared the castle wall.

Munch wasn't sure why until he took another step and the air closed around him, murky and thick as water. He struggled to breathe as he shoved each foot forward with a supreme effort.

Gritting his teeth, he reached down to his quiver and closed his fingers around the iron rod Robin insisted they keep handy. As his fingers touched the iron, some of the pressure eased, though he still had to fight for every step.

Will reached the wall and flinched as he touched the stone. "This whole place is guarded by fae magic."

John pounded his fist against the wall, grimacing and shaking out his hand moments later. "We have to get in."

"Perhaps we could try the gate?" Alan gestured in the direction of the main gate to the duke's castle.

"Likely locked up tight by fae magic as well, even if the guards would let us in." Will's jaw worked, and he faced the wall. "We'll have to climb it. We just have to get to that first window."

Munch swallowed. Trees were fine, but climbing walls wasn't his favorite thing. Especially not a wall actively warded by fae magic.

Will drew the iron rod from his quiver, bit down on it, hooked his bow over his shoulder, and wedged his fingers in the first handhold.

Munch drew his own iron rod from his quiver and clamped it between his teeth. He fought the gag reflex as the taste of iron filled his mouth. He started forward, but John shouldered him out of the way. At well over six foot and huge, John could do a lot of shouldering.

Before Munch could regain his balance, Tuck had also taken to the wall, an iron rod between his teeth and his favorite ladle in his belt.

Alan flashed Munch a grin before he too beat Munch to the wall.

As Munch stepped forward, Marion—only a year older than Munch—glared in a way that said Munch had better stay put. Since Marion had been forced to wear a dress very temporarily to play the part of the maid as part of this heist, he probably deserved the honor of climbing the wall next.

Finally it was Munch's turn. He took to the wall, digging his fingers and toes into the cracks between the large stones that formed the castle. The granite was thankfully firm and grippy, though sharp enough to scrape at his fingers with every move.

His fingers burned, his knees hurt from the number of times he'd bashed them into the castle wall.

"Keep your heads down," Will called from above a moment before glass shattered.

Munch pressed closer to the wall and tucked his face down to avoid getting broken glass into his eyes. A few shards pattered against his back, then he started upward once again.

A particularly sharp outcropping sliced at his palm, but he couldn't look at it to see how bad it was. The pressure of the fae magic was growing, and only the iron in his teeth was keeping it from sweeping him from the wall.

After another few feet, his hand brushed wood. Something clamped into the back of his shirt and hauled him upward. He rolled over the window frame, his body protected from the broken window by a rug thrown over the frame.

He barely staggered to his feet before Marion was shoving him forward. Will pulled open the door to the hallway, John and Tuck at his back. Munch trotted to keep up as they raced down the surprisingly empty hallways.

The overpowering fae magic built and built the deeper

they pressed into the castle. Munch flexed his fingers on the iron rod he'd stuffed back into his quiver. Each breath felt like the floral magic was stabbing into his lungs, swirling through his head. His stomach churned, and there was a strange ringing in his ears.

Then the whole world tilted. There wasn't an explosion, exactly, but something burst around them with a pop that twisted something inside him.

The fae magic swept away as if by a strong breeze. When Munch blinked, the once opulent hallway had turned shabby around him. The paintings were no longer vibrant, but dingy and dust covered. The red carpeting was now green and patchy and worn in places. The pedestals of decorations had disappeared completely.

Whatever that fae magic had been building towards, it had reached its climax.

Will shook himself, then pointed. "This way."

Together, they raced into a large room in the base of a tower. Mounted fae monsters filled the space with plaques labeling who had killed them. At the far side of the room, a tiny door was set into the wall underneath the staircase.

Will sprinted toward it, then tugged on the latch. "Locked. John?"

As soon as Will stepped out of the way, John gave the door a solid kick next to the latch. The door cracked and splintered around the latch, but it didn't fully open.

Together, Will and John rammed the door with their shoulders and burst inside the room.

Munch pressed against Alan and Marion's back, but he couldn't see anything as all of them crowded through the doorway. Ugh, he hated to be the littlest brother.

Finally, he stumbled into the room as the others stepped

aside and nearly tripped on the dead body lying near the door.

Sheriff Reinhault sprawled there with his eyes open, his long blond hair pooled on the floor, one of Robin's black-fletched arrows sticking out of his chest.

In the center of the room, Robin, her neck red and raw, knelt next to Duke Guy of Gysborn, pressing her hand to his bloody shoulder where one of her white-fletched practice arrows stuck out. A sisal noose lay on the floor next to her.

Will drew his sword. "Get away from her, Bluebeard."

"Will." Robin's voice came out a pained croak, so unlike her boisterous laugh. "Don't hurt him."

What was going on? Munch gaped from Robin to Duke Guy. Their sworn enemy. The man Robin had been trying to kill for seven years. The evil duke she'd married with plans to kill him before he killed her.

Yet even though she knelt there with the marks of a rope around her neck, it was Sheriff Reinhault who lay dead on the floor while Duke Guy was still alive. That was no accident. Robin was too good to have accidentally chosen a practice arrow when shooting Duke Guy. Nor would she have missed his heart by that much.

No, if Duke Guy was alive, then it was because Robin wanted him alive.

Even as Munch's mind whirled, he caught the last bit of Robin's and Will's conversation. "Reinhault is the one responsible for all of this. Look at him. He's *fae*."

Will whirled, but Munch was still standing there with the sheriff's body at his feet. In a daze, Munch knelt and gingerly pushed back the man's golden-blond hair, revealing the points of his tapered ears.

Munch's stomach lurched, and he stumbled backwards.

Sheriff Reinhault was a *fae*. After all these years of chasing and being chased by Duke Guy and his minion Sheriff Reinhault, it turned out that Reinhault was their true enemy all along.

They were foresters, or they had been before Duke Guy had disbanded the foresters. Not that Munch had ever been a true forester. He'd been eight when his parents had been killed, and nearly nine when the foresters were officially disbanded.

But Robin and Will had still made sure he was raised to know how to fight fae and their tricks. He'd still learned everything he needed to know to be a forester, even while he'd also learned how to be an outlaw.

What would this mean that a fae had been orchestrating everything?

MUNCH SNEAKED another glance at the darkness of the castle walltop beyond the blaze of the pyre where the coals burned Sheriff Reinhault's body to ash. But it was too dark for Munch to see Robin and Duke Guy where they had retreated to talk after they had given orders for the body to be burned.

The guards gave Munch and his brothers sidelong glances, but they didn't impede them or question their presence.

Soft footsteps sounded a moment before Robin and Duke Guy strolled from the darkness side by side. Far too cozy for Munch's liking. As if Robin intended to stay married to the duke.

The marriage had just been a part of the plot for the heist. Robin didn't actually like the duke, right?

Robin took in the pyre, the blackened ashes that were all that remained of the fae Reinhault. She gave a sharp nod, then faced the rest of them, planting her hands on her hips. "Good job on the pyre. Now, we need to talk." Her voice remained raspy, but not as bad as before. She flashed a cocky smile up at the duke. "Guy, can we use your study?"

"Of course." Duke Guy clasped his hands behind his back and lifted his gaze from Robin to take in his guards and the servants beyond. "Thank you all for your patience in waiting for an explanation of today's events. As you saw, Reinhault was a fae. He has held this castle captive in his glamour for the past ten years. Thanks to Lady Robin, the threat is now gone. I appreciate all of you standing by me despite the rumors and the strange happenings. Captain, please collect the ashes, place them in an iron box, then lock the box in one of the vaults."

The captain of the guard nodded and saluted his duke.

The duke gestured at Munch and the others. "These are my wife's brothers. Please prepare rooms for them."

"Near my room would be appreciated." Robin flashed that self-confident smile again.

The housekeeper nodded, then started shooing the maids and stableboys back to work or to bed, as the case might be.

Going to bed sounded like a great idea. Munch blinked and fought back a yawn, even as he trailed behind the others as Robin and Duke Guy led the way from the court-yard, into the castle, and down the hall to the duke's study.

Munch crowded inside, squishing against Marion's back to get far enough inside to shut the door. He would've thought his brothers would know to walk farther into the room to make room for everyone before they stopped, but no. Will and John had planted themselves just inside the door and didn't look ready to budge.

Robin hopped onto the desk, sitting on top of an open ledger and leaning back on her hands.

Duke Guy made a noise in the back of his throat and rubbed at his temple, pacing behind the desk rather than taking his seat behind it. "I am already regretting this."

"No, you're not. I'm growing on you." Robin grinned impishly up at the duke.

"Yes, like fungus on a tree." The duke scowled at her, his black hair and beard giving him a dark look in the flickering light of the candle. He halted behind the desk but still didn't take his seat.

Robin huffed and rolled her eyes. "Your humor is rather wooden. I'll have to work on that. Now." She swiveled on the desk, earning another noise from the duke, to better face the rest of them.

Munch eased along the wall so he wasn't so squished behind Marion. Whatever Robin was about to say was going to be momentous. As momentous as the day she announced they were going to turn outlaw to protect the village from the duke's malicious taxation.

"Guy knows I'm the Hood and that we're the outlaw gang who has been plaguing him for the past few years." Robin's face and voice held a strange solemnity for her. "He has promised to protect us from our past, and I've promised that we're done. The Hood is going to fade into legend."

"Then I can do whatever I want with the Hood stories, right?" Alan grinned and made a motion with his hands, as if he were strumming his lute.

"I'm counting on it." There was Robin's classic grin. "Even if I hang up my hood, I like to think that the Hood is still out there having adventures, even if I stay here as the dignified lady of the castle."

John snorted. "Dignified?"

Tuck smirked. "Lady?"

Will raised an eyebrow, though something in his gaze turned even more solemn. "You're staying?"

Robin drew in a deep breath and nodded. "Guy kind of likes me. I like annoying him. And I worked too hard to steal this castle to give it up. Of course I'm staying."

The duke opened his mouth, like he wanted to say something. Then he snapped his mouth shut again on a sigh.

Smart man. When Robin got on a roll like this, they all knew better than to interrupt with anything other than intelligent questions.

Munch kicked at the edge of the green rug. "So what happens to us?"

He'd been eleven when they'd taken to outlawry. He didn't really know any other life.

"We're free. You can do whatever you wish." Robin lounged back on her hands, as if entirely comfortable on top of the desk.

Duke Guy coughed. "Within the bounds of the law, of course."

"Well, yes. That, of course." Robin waved breezily. "I'm going to be the lady of the castle, so I should be able to get you any job you want. Tuck, if you want to work in the castle kitchens, I can make that happen. Alan, if you want to become a bard, you'll be welcome here until you can make a name for yourself."

Will dropped his hand to the iron bar in his quiver. "We

can't leave the faerie circles unguarded. Reinhault might be gone, but there are more fae and monsters that will come through."

"Reinhault said the monsters might actually get worse, now that he isn't here keeping them away." Robin met Will's gaze, then glanced at the duke. "The Greenwood still needs its foresters."

Duke Guy straightened his shoulders, clasping his hands behind his back. "You want me to trust outlaws with the protection of my forest?"

"We're the only trained foresters you've got." Robin poked the duke in the ribs, making him squirm in a way that broke his hard, correct posture. "Besides, we've been unofficially acting as foresters on top of being outlaws for the past few years. Just think of how much better a job we'll do with official resources."

"We?" Guy eased out of reach of her poking finger and crossed his arms over his stomach for added protection, a move Munch recognized since he'd employed it himself numerous times.

"Yes, *we*. If the monsters are going to be as bad as Reinhault claimed, then my brothers are going to need reinforcements." Robin shrugged. "Assuming any of my brothers want to volunteer to resume their roles as foresters."

Will huffed and crossed his arms. "Of course I will. I'm just surprised you won't be returning to the forest."

"Guy has promised to make life here interesting enough to make giving up the forest worth it." Robin sent another grin in the duke's direction.

The duke heaved another sigh. "I suppose that, as my lady, I can place you in charge of the foresters. Just keep in mind that my resources are rather limited at the moment. I will not be able to provide extravagantly for the reinstated foresters."

"If we're still answering to Robin instead of you, then I'm in." John hefted his quarterstaff.

"Good. If that's settled, then I'm off to bed." Robin hopped off the desk, shifting the papers out of their neat stacks while she was at it. "We don't have to make all our decisions for our new futures tonight."

That sounded like a good plan to Munch. All he wanted to do was sleep, and he didn't want to think about complicated things like futures and that their archenemy was apparently going to be their brother-in-law for real.

Robin sauntered between them. When none of them made a move for the door, she grinned back at them. "Don't hurt Guy too badly when you interrogate him. Remember, I only put a practice arrow into him. That's what I deemed to be our forester justice."

With that, Robin swept out of the room.

Leaving Munch and his brothers alone with Duke Guy. The man infamous for murdering his wives and who had hunted them for the past seven years.

Will crossed his arms, his stance taking on a hint of menace. "Why should we trust you? We saw the marks on her neck."

Duke Guy nudged the ledger back to straight on his desk, then faced them. He pressed a hand to his wounded shoulder. "You trusted Robin enough to follow her orders. Do you trust her judgment in this?"

Well, the duke had them there. Munch found a more comfortable spot to lean against the wall. He was the youngest. His opinion wasn't going to count for much, even if he did voice it. He might as well let the others take charge, as they always did.

Will huffed, but he took another step closer to crowd the duke. Duke Guy stood a few inches taller than Will, though John was taller yet. Will met the duke's gaze. "Yes, I trust Robin. But know this. If you hurt our sister—"

"She will kill me before any of you do." Duke Guy held Will's gaze without flinching.

Will opened his mouth, hesitated, then his stance relaxed. "True. Fine, if you hurt Robin, we'll help her bury your body out in the forest where no one will ever find it."

"You have my word. I will keep Robin safe." Guy returned to his stiff, hands-clasped-behind-his-back stance.

Alan snorted. "If you can keep Robin safe, then you'd be the first. I wish you luck with that."

The corner of the duke's mouth might have twitched, but it was hard to tell beneath his thick black beard.

Then his gaze hardened once again. "While I do not have the authority to pardon you, I am prepared to shield Robin and all of you from your past activities as outlaws. Robin has given her word that she is done, but I would like your promises as well."

Will smirked. "You trusted Robin enough to take her word for it. She's promised that we're done, so we're done."

"Just like that?" Duke Guy's dark eyes searched Will's face, then swept over the rest of them.

"Just like that." Will stated it with a finality that spoke for all of them.

Alan shrugged. "We became outlaws because Robin announced it one day. We'll stop being outlaws the same way. It's how we work."

Duke Guy held his stance for a moment longer before

his shoulders slumped. "I thought Robin was the crazy one, but I'm beginning to think your whole family is a bit touched."

"You have to be a little feral to be a forester and take on the fae." Will turned away from the duke, heading for the door.

"Though Robin is the craziest of all of us." Alan grinned and smoothed the front of his shirt as if he already envisioned himself in a bard's get-up.

"Yeah. Crazy like an old fox who has figured out how to steal the rabbits right out of the snare," Tuck muttered under his breath before he fell in beside Will.

At the door, Will turned, glancing back at the duke. "One hint about our sister. If she gets bored, she can get a little…"

"Stir crazy," John finished for Will.

"Reckless," Tuck added.

"Annoying." Munch shuddered. The last time they'd gone too long between stealing tax collection shipments, Robin had gotten them up insanely early in the morning just to run extra forester drills.

"Destructive," Marion muttered under his breath.

"Crazy. Just crazy," Alan said with a long-suffering sigh.

"I will…keep that in mind." That quirk returned to Duke Guy's mouth. "Now, gentlemen, your rooms should be ready. I think we should retire for the night."

Will led the way out the door, but then he stopped just a little ways down the hallway. He had something on his mind that he didn't want Duke Guy to overhear.

Stomach rumbling, Munch found a new position along the wall and reached into his pocket, fishing out the piece of bread. It was rather smushed after the night's events, but it would still stop the gurgling. He took a bite, chewing while he waited for Will to get to the point.

Duke Guy stepped out of his study, locked it behind him, and glanced at them. Something flickered in his hard expression, almost like an eye roll even if he didn't do anything that drastic, before he strode down the hall toward the tower that held his room.

Once Duke Guy was out of earshot, Will faced them. "John, Tuck, return to the forest. I don't like leaving the Greenwood unguarded, especially now that we know we had one fae under our noses this entire time. Marion, you and I will guard Robin's room tonight. Alan, Munch—" Will turned to him. "Guard Duke Guy. I know Robin said he's trustworthy, but I'd feel better knowing he doesn't leave his room tonight."

Alan flourished a salute, then nudged Munch's arm. "Stop munching and come on."

Munch came, though he didn't stop munching. Who knew when he'd get fed again? He wasn't sure how food worked in this castle, especially since he didn't know if they were guests or family or just outlaws who Duke Guy would arrest once he was done toying with all of them.

They strode through the castle at a much more leisurely pace than they'd done earlier in the night. This time when they reached the room filled with stuffed and mounted magical monsters, they headed up the winding staircase, passing the small room where they'd found Robin and Duke Guy earlier, the door still hanging open, the latch splintered.

At the top of the stairs, two guards crowded the landing before a closed door. The guard on the left dropped his hand to his sword's hilt. "What are you doing here?"

Alan grinned and crossed his arms. "We're here to help guard the duke. We're foresters. We are experts in dealing with the fae."

"The fae is now dead. Go back to your forest. That's where you belong." The guard stepped a little farther in front of the door, raising his voice.

"We have guards in the forest already, never fear." Alan's grin never wavered. "But I'm under orders to guard the duke."

"Well, I am under orders to keep the duke from being disturbed." The guard's voice rose as his fellow guard gripped his sword as if about to draw it. "Now move along before we move you out of here."

As the guard took a menacing step forward, the door behind him yanked open. The duke stood there, dressed in only his trousers and his shirt half-unbuttoned as if he had been readying himself for bed when the raised voices had drawn his attention. "What is the meaning of this?"

Both guards straightened. The guard on the left swiveled to better face his duke and keep Alan and Munch in view. "These two men claim they are here to guard you."

Duke Guy glanced at Alan and Munch, then sighed. "I suppose they are. Thank you for your diligence, Rogers. You two—" The duke motioned to Alan and Munch. "You can bunk in my sitting room. If you must."

"We must." Alan kept flashing that grin as he pushed past Duke Guy into the duke's sitting room.

Munch took a step, then hesitated as the duke swung his dark, forbidding eyes onto him. The only glare Munch feared more was Robin's. And maybe Will's. And, well, John's. And...and Munch had far too many big brothers. The last thing he needed was yet another one glaring at him.

After a moment, Duke Guy spun on his heel and marched back into the sitting room.

With another glance at the guards, Munch scurried past and entered the room.

"Close the door." Duke Guy never broke his stride as he crossed the room. "And do not disturb me before breakfast." The door to his bedroom slammed shut in his wake.

Alan flopped onto the couch which was so worn that the pattern in the green fabric was no longer discernible. "I claim the couch."

Munch sighed. Of course he did. That left Munch with his choice of one of the cushioned chairs or the floor.

With another sigh, he grabbed a pillow from one of the chairs and stretched out on the floor in front of the bedroom door. At least that way he could get some sleep while making sure the duke didn't leave his room.

Just as he was getting settled in—the rug over stone was less comfortable than his cushy bed of pine boughs and moss out in the forest—the door beside him opened. He tilted his head to peer up at the duke looming over him.

The duke's dour frown didn't waver as he dropped a blanket onto Munch, then tossed a second blanket to Alan. Without a word, Duke Guy shut the door yet again, the lock clicking into place.

Not that the lock would do him much good. Even Munch could pick it if he wished, though he wasn't nearly as quick at it as Robin or an expert like Will.

But that likely wasn't the point. The duke would tolerate them only so far. If they respected that, then he would afford them a measure of respect in return.

Wrapping the blanket over his shoulder, Munch settled in to try to get some rest without the warble of crickets, burble of tree frogs, and sighing of the nighttime forest to lull him to sleep.

MUNCH BLINKED BLEARILY as a pounding noise reverberated above him. He groaned and squinted upward. When he caught sight of his sister, he groaned again and squeezed his eyes shut. Just that glimpse told him she was in an annoying mood this morning.

Robin leaned over him, pounding on the door to the duke's bedroom. She flashed a grin down at him but kept hammering on the door with her fist.

Munch rolled to his hands and knees and crawled out of there. No way did he want to find himself lying on the floor when the duke opened the door.

He'd only made it partially out of the way, the blanket draped around him, when the door whooshed open.

Duke Guy leaned heavily against the doorframe, his black hair and beard tousled and sticking up at all angles, altogether different than his normally groomed and polished appearance. He wore the same trousers as yesterday, but he lacked a shirt so that the bandage over his shoulder was visible. "Robin. What are you doing here? The sun is barely up."

"We have things to do, foresters to reinstate, a castle to set to rights." Robin grinned and leaned against the door across from Duke Guy. "We aren't going to do all that by lazing in bed."

"We won't accomplish it on lack of sleep either." Duke Guy swiped a hand over his face, as if still trying to wake up.

Munch agreed with the duke—little as he wanted to admit it—but after years of jumping to Robin's orders, he was used to her early morning wake up calls. He crawled a few more inches out of the way.

Alan still sprawled on the couch, eyes closed. The slight twitch of a smile gave away that he was awake, even if he was pretending to sleep to avoid getting rousted into action by Robin.

"You got plenty of sleep." Robin huffed and flicked her fingers at Duke Guy's chest without touching him. "Now, go put on a shirt."

Munch eased to his feet along the wall. Only a few more inches, and he would be out of Robin's and Guy's line of sight. Then he could make a run for it. Would the kitchen have started breakfast by now? That bread he'd nibbled on before bed was a long time ago.

Duke Guy smoothed a hand over his beard, a hint of a smile on his mouth as he met Robin's gaze. "What if I can't put on a shirt thanks to my wound?"

Robin smirked at him, her gaze sweeping over him, then the bandage, before focusing on his face. "I suppose you want me to offer to help?"

"Would you if I asked?" Duke Guy's gaze held an extra heat.

Munch slid farther along the wall. He did *not* want to be here. He had never seen his sister flirt before, and it was downright uncomfortable seeing it now. If that sharp-edged smirk of hers could be considered flirting.

Yes, Duke Guy was her husband, and she hadn't killed him yet so she must actually like him. But he had been their archenemy. They'd spent the last seven years trying to kill him and avoiding getting killed by him. It was beyond strange to suddenly have him as one of the family.

Robin's smirk widened.

Munch slid another step along the wall. Just another few inches, and he would be safe.

Robin's hand latched onto his sleeve and yanked him backwards. Munch stumbled and, before he could regain his balance, Robin shoved him through the doorway. Her smirk widened. "Munch can help you. See you both at breakfast."

Robin shut the door in their faces.

Munch clutched the blanket around his shoulders and faced Duke Guy. His enemy. His brother-in-law. He didn't even know anymore.

Guy heaved another sigh. "Who is she trying to torment? You or me?"

"Both, I think." Munch grimaced as his stomach grumbled. Couldn't Robin wait to get annoying until after he'd gotten breakfast?

"Hmm." Guy gave a grunt and crossed the room. He opened the wardrobe, his stance and expression going all stiff again, as he held his injured arm tightly against his chest. "I have no need of your assistance."

Fine by Munch. He leaned against the door and took in the room. Worn, green rugs covered most of the floor while a darker green blanket lay rumpled on the bed. An ornate mantel rested above the fireplace while wood paneling warmed what would have been stone walls otherwise.

The duke pulled clothes out of the wardrobe, hiding behind one of the doors as he changed.

Munch resisted the urge to snort at that. Definitely an only child. The duke had clearly never had to share a cave bedroom with five older brothers, getting all their hand-me-downs and having to watch out for shirts snapped at his skin while changing.

The duke gave a pained grunt. "You are the youngest, correct? Forgive me, but what is your name again?"

Munch hesitated for two reasons. First, it seemed dangerous to give his former enemy—still not sure on the former part—his name. Especially one who had been under the power of a fae for years.

But second and the most important reason was his name was…embarrassing. Beyond embarrassing.

"Yes. My name is Mungoe," Munch muttered, half-hoping that Guy wouldn't be able to hear.

"Mungoe?" Guy paused and glanced around the wardrobe door at him.

"I go by Munch." Munch crossed his arms. Why couldn't his parents have given the name to Alan? Alan was the bard of the family. He would have appreciated being named after a character of their mother's favorite story.

But, no, Munch had been the one stuck with a moniker so embarrassing that he preferred a nickname like "Munch."

"Hmm." This time, Guy's non-committal hum turned into a pained noise in the back of his throat. "You're sixteen? Seventeen?"

Ugh, really? The duke was attempting the whole brother-in-law bonding thing now? As if Munch needed yet another brother. Especially one who was something like thirty-four or five years old. That made Guy *old*. Closer in age to Munch's late parents than to Munch.

Munch scowled at the duke. "Eighteen. And I already have five big brothers. I don't need another one bossing me around."

If anything, the awkward stiffness to the room deepened. "I see." Guy's tone returned to that short, ducal one he usually used. "I will not attempt to be your brother or *boss you around*. But you have been raised by outlaws, and I will hold you and your brothers to the standard of the law."

What did Robin see in this guy? He was so utterly stiff, law-abiding, and humorless. The exact opposite of Robin.

Perhaps she saw a challenge.

Of course she saw a challenge. Somewhere between nearly getting hanged and telling them that she was hanging up her outlaw cloak, she had decided that her new mission in life was to turn Guy's life upside down.

Munch smirked and leaned against the wall behind him. If he was going to stop being an outlaw, at least this new life would be entertaining. "Robin is going to twist you into knots."

"Nothing new there." Guy gave another grunt of pain as he tried to pull on a black shirt. After another stifled moan, Guy sighed and stepped around the wardrobe door, his mouth tight. "I must beg for your help after all."

Munch sighed too and pushed away from the wall. He really should have stashed more bread in his pockets if his breakfast was going to be this delayed. "Fine. I've had to help Will before when he was recovering from an arrow wound. Come to think of it, you were the one who put the arrow into him, weren't you?"

Approaching the duke, gripping his wrist, and maneuvering his arm into his sleeve was a whole lot more awkward than doing it for Will. The duke might order him beheaded for the pain he was causing.

Duke Guy winced, but he didn't resist or pull away. As soon as he slid his arm through his sleeve, he held his arm stiffly, a white pallor to his face.

Munch located the sling set aside on the chair, then helped Guy work it over his head and settle his injured arm into it. He stepped back and stuck his hands into his pockets. Nope, no bits of bread left. "Now can we get breakfast?"

Guy leaned against the wardrobe for a moment, dragging in a deep breath, before he straightened. He strode toward the door, then paused, glancing back at Munch. His expression twisted, as if the words hurt. "Thank you for your assistance."

"Don't mention it. You know I only helped because Robin ordered me to." Munch trudged toward the door.

"Still, thank you." Guy gave Munch another hard, disapproving look. "Gratitude is the polite reaction to help, even if that help was reluctantly given."

Munch snorted and gave a shrug-nod gesture since Guy seemed to expect some kind of reaction. Guy, apparently, was going to take his new big brother role very seriously, despite none of them needing him.

Oh, well. Munch wasn't sure what his new not-outlaw life would look like, but it would be entertaining to watch Robin ruffle Duke Guy's feathers as his wife instead of his adversary.

The First Kiss

Chapter One

Brigid dodged the rapier that the swordmaiden Minnie swung at her head. Minnie, a goblin fae with long cattle horns and cow ears poking through her long, light brown hair, swung again with all the power of her toned arms, far more used to swinging her two-handed broadsword than the smaller rapier.

Brigid jumped back, trying to put space between herself and her opponent. She couldn't overpower Minnie, nor could she outfight her. While Brigid had been training with the swordmaidens for two years, many of the swordmaidens had been training for far longer. Not to mention that swordfighting didn't come naturally to her. She'd much rather pick out a pretty dress than a pretty sword.

But she had her wits, and her wits had to be her greatest weapon, no matter what weapon she had in her hand.

She dodged another thrust.

Minnie growled in the back of her throat. "Come on. Stand and fight like a swordmaiden for once."

"I think not." Brigid ducked again, swinging up with her

rapier and managing to knock Minnie's blade aside more by accident than on purpose. "You'll clobber me if I try."

"But you'll never win if you always run." Minnie pressed forward, chopping at Brigid's head.

Brigid yelped as she brought her arms up, blocking the chop more by accident than anything else. She'd even closed her eyes. A bad habit she couldn't seem to break when she fought.

Before Minnie could press the advantage, Brigid threw herself a few steps backwards. "Yes, but I won't lose either."

Across the large, stone training pavilion, swordmaidens grunted and sweated through their various training routines. Some sparred with swords, others with spears. Beyond the white pillars bordering the pavilion, other swordmaidens practiced their archery as they galloped across a field on snorting, fire-maned unicorns.

Minnie lunged, and Brigid ran, ducking for cover behind one of the pillars. What could she do to gain the advantage? She wasn't as strong or as skilled as Minnie. She'd just have to be clever.

As Minnie sprang around the pillar, Brigid didn't lunge away this time. Instead, she stuck out her foot, tripping Minnie. Before Minnie could regain her balance, Brigid pressed the edge of her own rapier to Minnie's throat. "Got you."

Sort of. Minnie still had her sword in her hand, so it wasn't a great win. But it was something.

The tip of something sharp and cold pricked Brigid's jaw beneath her ear. "Trying to be clever again, Brigid, instead of actually learning how to use your sword?"

Bothersome bats, she had forgotten to remain wary of her surroundings.

Brigid sighed and sheathed her rapier, turning to face Queen Hippolyta. "It worked, didn't it?"

"Clever, but not clever enough is still going to end with you dead." Queen Hippolyta lowered her own sword, a larger, double-bladed weapon with a glinting blade and hilt decorated with just a hint of gold filigree. "Thank you for your assistance today, Minnie."

Minnie bowed to her queen before she raced to the weapons rack, swapping the rapier for her normal broadsword. With a roar that sounded more like jubilation than a war cry, Minnie threw herself into a squad of training swordmaidens.

Brigid sighed and gestured in that direction. "I'm not like them. I'm never going to love training or fighting."

"I'm not asking you to be an intimidating warrior woman like them." Queen Hippolyta gave her practicing warriors a fond smile before she speared Brigid with a sharp look in her light blue eyes. "You have been training with my swordmaidens for two years now. You know that there is more to being a swordmaiden than fighting. Some of my swordmaidens fight by being warriors, and, yes, those are the swordmaidens I often send to the other courts to perpetuate the image that all my warriors are big, brawny, and the stereotypical female warrior."

That was true, and Brigid had seen plenty of examples of swordmaidens who fought with a variety of weapons, from the sneaky assassin swordmaidens to the archers to those who, like her, favored smaller weapons.

And while they exuded intimidation on the outside, Brigid had learned even the biggest and brawniest had hidden depths below the curated image. Even now, several of the swordmaidens sported elaborate hairstyles or jewelry as they practiced. Minnie was a softie who would burst into tears at both the exceptionally happy and tear-jerking sad parts of a play. Ariadne appeared icy on the outside but could giggle over makeup and hairstyles with the best of them.

Queen Hippolyta waved at her swordmaidens again. "Some of my swordmaidens fight with words. Or, like you, with their wits. But all of them must know how to defend themselves and others. It is the purpose of the Court of Swordmaidens. Those who do not wish to meet my requirements are free to settle elsewhere."

Brigid nodded, rubbing her thumb on the hilt of her sword. Technically, she wasn't a swordmaiden. She was on a temporary loan to Queen Hippolyta from the queen's husband King Theseus. While Brigid trained with the swordmaidens, she was still a member of the Court of Knowledge, where the rest of her family lived.

Queen Hippolyta lifted her sword again, though she didn't menace Brigid. "By all means, wear the pretty dresses you favor. But I will make sure you know how to move—and fight—in a dress so that the skirts don't impede your movements and you don't trip on the hem."

Brigid sighed and smoothed a hand down the short, fluttering skirt she currently wore. "I suppose that would be helpful."

Even if she never got into sword fights, knowing how to properly walk in a fancy dress was going to be important. She had grown up dirt poor on a failing farm in the Human Realm. She had never worn anything fancier than well-worn muslin until she'd come to the Fae Realm two years ago.

Queen Hippolyta stepped closer to Brigid. "My swordmaidens have each other. They live together. Fight together. Win together. Their strength is in their sisterhood. But you, I'm afraid, will fight alone. Even when you gather allies, you will not be able to call on them without revealing them. Because you fight in the shadows, you will likely be alone when the time to fight comes."

"I have a feeling that if it comes to a fight, then I've already failed." Brigid rested her hand on the hilt of her rapier.

"Perhaps. But you will fail eventually. Everyone does." Queen Hippolyta took a step back and raised her sword again. "Draw your sword."

Brigid suppressed a groan and drew her sword. If fighting Minnie had been bad, fighting Queen Hippolyta was going to be so much worse. She was going to get her butt kicked to the edge of the Realm of Monsters and back, and that would be if Queen Hippolyta went easy on her.

QUEEN HIPPOLYTA DIDN'T GO easy.

At least, it hadn't felt easy to Brigid. She limped up the stairs from the practice pavilion to the white palace perched on the hill above the crystalline turquoise of the sea far below. Every muscle ached, and her arms hung limply at her sides. When she passed other swordmaidens on their way down, she just nodded to them since she didn't have the energy to lift her hand in acknowledgement.

Why were there so many stairs? Brigid found herself breathing hard before she even got halfway up them, her legs burning after all the training and exercise she'd done before tackling the stairs.

Some of the swordmaidens who had passed her on their way down now passed her again on their way up as they jogged the stairs. Training-crazy swordmaidens.

Finally, Brigid stepped into the palace, which felt airy despite being built of stone thanks to all the white marble and the many rooms which were completely open to the warm summer breezes that wafted from the sea, the benefits of being an island kingdom of the Summer Courts where perpetual summer reigned.

She walked through the palace and its lush gardens until she reached the far side, where this court's Anywhere Door had been built into the side of a hill surrounded by another columned pavilion. She nodded at the two swordmaidens who guarded the Door, but neither of them moved to stop her.

Setting her hand on the latch, she pictured where she wanted to go. Then she opened the Door and stepped through, instantly going from the breezy, seaside palace in the Court of Swordmaidens into the white columned Hall of Anywhere Doors in the Court of Knowledge.

The hall bustled with fae on their way to ask questions of the librarians or to request a book or to spend a few hours curled in a cushy corner, reading their chosen book.

Brigid drew in a deep breath of the forest and leather smell of the Great Library that filled even this hall of marble and doors. She might not have become a librarian like the rest of her siblings, but over the past two years she had learned to love this Library. Not as much as Basil, but few people loved this Library as much as Basil did.

She strolled through the hall, waved at the swordmaidens guarding the doors, and stepped inside the Great Library itself.

A large tree dominated the Library's atrium while the master librarians in their black coats worked behind their desks at its base. The assistant librarians in green coats bustled about, looking up books and answers. A few apprentice librarians scurried about as well in their gray uniforms. They were mostly young fae who hadn't yet earned their way into the position of assistant librarian. Somewhere in the Library, Brigid's siblings Viola, Sebastian, and Beatrice wore gray uniforms while they worked, either running errands or working in the book repair room.

Brigid strolled through the winding aisles of bookshelves, occasionally reaching out to tap one of the Library's branches or scratch a bookwyrm behind the ruff.

When she reached the book repair room, she swept inside, a grin already on her face. Only Viola sat at the table, stitching a binding back together. Not too surprising, since Basil and Meg were gone in the Human Realm, tracking down something for King Theseus and Queen Hippolyta. Sebastian must still be at his own sword practice here in the Court of Knowledge with King Theseus's nobles.

Brigid plopped into the seat across from Viola. "Where's Beatrice?"

"Brigid!" Viola glanced up from the book she was sewing back together. Her blonde hair, lighter than Brigid's brown-blonde, flowed over her shoulders. "Beatrice was…"

With a huff, Beatrice stomped into the room, a bookwyrm perched on her shoulder and a stack of damaged books in her arms. "Ugh! He's so *awful!*"

Viola sighed. "Benedict again? What did he do this time?"

Beatrice juggled the books, then lifted a section of her hair, showing where the light blonde strands changed from their normal color to chartreuse. "He dipped my hair in giant talking snail slime."

Brigid winced. That was going to be hard even for the House's magic grotto to get out. Even once they got the slime out of Beatrice's hair, that section would probably be dyed green for a while. The giant talking snails from the Swamp Court left behind some nasty sludge. "Don't worry, Beatrice. I'm sure we can get most of it out."

Brigid might have to help plot a prank in return to get Benedict back for pranking her sister. That was the fae way, after all. Benedict might be the son of one of King Theseus's nobles, but that didn't give him the right to torment her sister.

"But it's giant talking snail slime." Beatrice slouched into one of the other chairs. "It won't come out."

Viola pushed to her feet. "Go home and start washing it out. I'll look up giant talking snail slime in the library. If there's a way to get it out, the Library will have the answer."

"You might want to try both the section on the Swamp Court and the section on the properties of magical species." Basil's voice rang from the doorway.

Brigid glanced up, smiling at the sight of her brother-in-law Basil cradling his and Meg's four-month-old daughter Addy in a carrier against his chest. Next to him, Meg reached over and wiped a line of drool off Addy's face before it could sully Basil's black librarian coat.

Beatrice dumped the bookwyrm and the damaged books onto the table, hopped to her feet, and raced to Basil and Meg. She wrapped her arms around both of them and hugged them. "You're home! You didn't get stuck in the Human Realm!"

"Of course we didn't. The faerie circle was a little more

interesting to navigate without Buddy's help, but we didn't get too lost." Meg patted Beatrice's back, avoiding the giant talking snail slime. Then she reached out to touch Addy's chubby cheek. "Addy took to the travel like a chicken to cracked corn."

Brigid grinned and reached over Beatrice to tug Addy free from the carrier. Her niece had the most adorable dark brown hair, chubby cheeks, slightly tapered ears, and the brightest smile in the world.

Addy smiled and gripped Brigid's dress as she settled against her side. Brigid bounced her niece on her hip a bit. "Of course Addy did. She's a sweetheart."

"She is also a part of both realms." Meg's eyes held a proud warmth. "Perhaps that has something to do with it."

Basil shrugged out of the baby carrier and stuffed it in a pocket of his coat. Due to the magical nature of the coat pockets, the carrier didn't make so much as a bulge as it disappeared.

Basil gestured toward the door. "Viola, would you like my help with searching the Great Library for what it has on giant talking snail slime?"

Viola smiled and hurried past him. "Yes!"

Of all of them, Viola and Sebastian had developed the deepest love for the Library. The two of them were determined to train with Basil so that they could earn green assistant librarian coats as soon as they were old enough.

"Wait for me!" Beatrice trotted after them, the bookwyrm slithering after her. "Can you walk with me to the Anywhere Door? I don't want Benedict to get a chance to dump more slime on my head."

Brigid bounced Addy on her hip again and turned to Meg. "How was the trip, really?"

"It was nice spending some time in the Human Realm again." Meg strode farther into the room, halting next to the long book repair table. "We just finished reporting to King Theseus. We found one of the three fae who were banished from the Court of Revels years ago. He'd lured the Duke of Gysborn into a terrible bargain and caused the drought over the whole kingdom."

Brigid didn't realize her grip on Addy had tightened until the baby squirmed in her arms. She forced herself to relax as she bounced Addy. "A fae caused the drought? He's the reason…"

She couldn't finish. One of those three fae that had King Theseus so worried had caused the drought. The same drought that had caused the deaths of their parents, forced them to mortgage the farm to Cullen, and eventually compelled them to leave the Human Realm entirely.

Brigid drew in a deep breath. All right. So a fae was at fault. All the more reason for her mission. She was eighteen now. Surely it was time to stop training and start rescuing.

Someone had to do it. The fae had been taking advantage of humans for too long.

Meg leaned back against the table and met Brigid's gaze. "We also found what you have been looking for. People in the Human Realm who can help with your mission."

"Really?" Brigid took a few more steps toward her sister. This could be her chance. Surely Queen Hippolyta would finally have to give her leave to begin her clandestine activities if she saw that Brigid had a league ready and willing to help.

Addy squirmed and wiggled to be let down.

Brigid laid Addy down by their feet, and Addy dug her fingers into the mossy floor with a giggle. "Do you truly think they'll help? It will be dangerous. Most humans don't want to take on the fae."

"Do you remember those legends about the foresters of the Greenwood?" Meg focused on Addy, her smile at odds with the serious tone in her voice. "Turns out they're real. The duke of Gysborn and his wife oversee the foresters, and they protect their part of the forest from fae and fae monsters. They know more about the fae, faerie circles, and how to defeat rogue fae than anyone I've ever met."

"Sounds like exactly the kind of allies I'll need." Brigid's heart pounded harder. She had spent two years training for this with some of the best warriors the fae had.

But humans who trained to take on the fae? Now that was the kind of training Brigid would need. These human foresters could teach her things that even Queen Hippolyta might not know—or want to share with a human.

Meg held Brigid's gaze. "I know. Basil and I mentioned you and your mission. We set up a way to stay in contact, but it will mean sneaking into the section of the Tanglewood that belongs to the Court of Revels."

Of course it would. Meg and Basil had gone through a thin spot on that side of the Tanglewood, which had dumped them out in a different part of the Greenwood than the thin spot on this side of the Tanglewood.

"I'll need to leave as soon as possible." Brigid dropped her voice, her throat aching a bit. Basil and Meg hadn't stayed long in the Human Realm. But what if Brigid decided to stay longer to receive training from these foresters? How much time would pass in the Human Realm before she returned to her family?

It didn't matter. This was her chosen mission. She would pursue this no matter the sacrifices.

Chapter Two

Munch was bored.

He munched on an apple as he strolled through the Greenwood, walking the patrol that his older brother Will had assigned to him. Of course, it happened to be the safest—and thus most boring—patrol in all of the Greenwood. That was what happened when one had five older brothers—and an older sister—and they all saw him as the baby of the family.

Well, he was eighteen. Almost nineteen, now. Far from a baby. Surely it was about time his family realized that.

But to them, he was just Munch. The boy they had raised after their parents had been killed by fae.

Munch inspected the apple core, but there wasn't much left to eat, unless he started gnawing on it like a squirrel. With a sigh, he tossed the core into the forest, then patted his pockets. What else had he brought along to eat? He'd already eaten the slice of bread, cheese, and meat earlier that day. And the scone he'd swiped from the kitchens.

Hmm. All he had left was the packet of venison jerky

he'd stuffed into his pocket two days ago. It was jerky. It would still be fine. And he did like jerky. But it was annoying when it got stuck in his teeth, and he was craving something sweeter.

Oh, well. He'd walk for another half an hour before he got out a piece of jerky. He had to make it last until that evening, and it was only early afternoon.

He trudged a few more steps, last fall's leaves crunching underfoot. All around him, the forest glowed with the bright green of late spring, not yet burnt by the heat of summer. A few of the lower parts of the forest held puddles of water, and he weaved around the damp spot to avoid leaving footprints. Not that he had to worry about leaving tracks for Duke Guy's men to find, but it was habit at this point.

Hmm. Perhaps he'd get the venison jerky out in twenty minutes.

No, make that fifteen.

Actually, the next faerie circle was just ahead. He'd inspect it, then he'd dig out the jerky.

Munch strolled through the forest, and the circle grew visible between the broad trunks of the oaks and maples.

This circle was formed of eerily identical red capped mushrooms arranged in a perfect circle around a tiny clearing in the forest. Inside the circle, grass grew far too green and dense for the forest and a heaviness of magic pressed into the surrounding forest with a floral stickiness he could taste.

Yet as he approached, something inside the circle shimmered, and the weight of magic pressed down even heavier until a headache built at his temples.

His heart hammered harder, and he fumbled to draw an

arrow from his quiver at his hip. No, wait, his bow wasn't even strung. He dropped the arrow as he ripped the unstrung bow from his back and scrambled to bend it to slip the bowstring into place.

Something was coming through the circle, and he wasn't ready.

Forget danger. A nice, boring stroll through the Greenwood wasn't so bad after all. Could he just go back to that?

The bowstring slid into place, and he swiped the arrow from the ground with trembling fingers.

He hadn't been this jumpy around the circles, back when he and his siblings had been using them to evade Duke Guy.

But ever since the evil fae Reinhault had been killed, monsters had been pouring through the circles with alarming frequency. Worse, Munch's family had found out the truth of how their parents had died.

If his parents, trained and experienced foresters as they had been, had been killed by a fae, then what chance did Munch stand if another fae like Reinhault was coming through this circle? He was by himself, miles from any of his siblings. He had his signal horn, but would he have a chance to get it out if he were attacked? Fae could put a human under their glamour far too easily, unless one had iron on hand for protection.

Iron. Of course. What had he been thinking?

Munch held the bow and arrow in his left hand, then reached for his quiver again. His seeking fingers landed on the iron rod that all foresters carried near to hand for just this purpose.

How was Munch supposed to hold the iron rod while drawing his bow and arrow?

The magic pressure grew worse. The shimmer was so hazy that he couldn't see to the other side. Whoever or whatever was coming through would be there at any moment.

Munch stuck the iron rod in his mouth, gripping it in his teeth like he was a pirate in those stories Alan told about the buccaneers plaguing the Sether Sea to the far south of the kingdom. Saliva collected in his mouth, and he slurped around the iron rod to keep his spit from drooling out of his mouth and onto his chin. That would look really intimidating if he found himself facing a fae.

Placing his back to a tree, Munch nocked the arrow, adjusted his grip on his bow, and forced himself to take long, deep breaths through his nose to steady his heart and his hands. He'd never get off a good shot if he let his fear get the best of him like this.

He was a forester. The little brother of the notorious Hood. He could handle whatever came through that faerie circle.

A hazy shape appeared in the circle a moment before the magic burst like a bubble popping at the surface of a boiling pot. The ambient magic subsided to its usual simmer, and a girl stepped from the ring of mushrooms.

Her golden-brown hair caught the glints of light coming through the forest canopy and framed the oval of her face. The light pink dress she wore fluttered around her knees in a style he'd never seen before outside of that brief visit by that human who had married a fae. This girl looked to be no older than he was, all slender and graceful and…

And the prettiest girl he'd ever seen.

He found himself relaxing his grip on his bow.

Wait, no. What was he doing? This must be a glamour. She was a fae. She must be bewitching him somehow.

He raised his bow and whirled out from behind the tree, keeping the tree's solid bulk at his back.

The girl gave a yip of surprise and raised her hands, her eyes going wide. Eyes which, he now could see, were brown like his, but far lighter and almost amber.

No, don't get lost in her eyes. She was a fae. She was dangerous.

Munch kept his stance menacing, though he didn't draw the arrow back just yet. Robin had always been very stern that one only drew the arrow when one was ready to shoot whatever one aimed at. And he wasn't ready to shoot this girl just yet.

He tried to ask her who she was and what she was doing there, only to remember that he still held the iron rod in his mouth. His words came out garbled around the iron, and a line of drool escaped despite his best efforts. It worked its way down his chin, then onto his neck.

Well, that was embarrassing.

She kept her hands raised, but she slowly reached with her left hand and swept her hair behind her ear, revealing a rounded, human ear. "I'm not a fae. My name is Brigid. I'm here to see Duke Guy of Gysborn and his wife Robin. My sister Meg and her husband Basil were here—actually, I'm not sure how long ago they were here. They returned to the Fae Realm yesterday, but I'm not sure how much time has passed here in the meantime."

Munch hesitated. She could be lying. She could be hiding the tips of her ears with a glamour. And he might not be able to sense the glamour, standing as close to the more powerful magic of the faerie circle as they were now.

But Robin had declared that Meg and Basil were trustworthy. And it was unlikely the two of them had told many people of their visit here.

They could have been captured and tortured by some unknown villain in the Fae Realm, for all Munch knew. Wouldn't they have sent word that their sister was coming?

Although, the tree that Robin and Meg had decided to use to pass messages lay in another circle in the part of the Greenwood that Will was currently patrolling. There might be a message there, and Will wouldn't have had time to get word to Munch to expect a visitor. With the way time worked between the two realms, Brigid might even have arrived before the note warning of her arrival.

Or was it all a trick? How was Munch to know? If he made the wrong decision, he could end up dead. Worse, he could set another conniving fae loose on the Greenwood, leading to another decade of drought and death.

More drool poured out of his mouth around the iron rod before he could suck it back in. Well, this wasn't working. And there was one way to test if she was really human or not.

With a glance in her direction, Munch slid the arrow back into his quiver, then took the iron rod from his mouth. As subtly as he could, he swiped his sleeve across his face to wipe away the spit.

He strode toward her, and she leaned back, as if she were prepared to bolt.

"Touch this." Munch held the iron rod out to her. The middle of it still shone wetly, and as soon as he tilted the iron rod toward her, a bead of his spit ran down the iron onto the side he'd asked her to touch.

Um, well, this was embarrassing. She must find him

gross. Would it be better to take back the iron rod to wipe it off or pretend he didn't see the spit and ignore it?

The girl gave a small, tentative laugh. "And here I thought we had strange customs in the Fae Realm." She reached out and wrapped her fingers around the iron without so much as a flinch.

She wouldn't have been able to touch the iron without severe pain if she'd been a fae. Unless she either was willingly married to a human, the way Basil was, or had performed blood rites, the way Reinhault had.

Maybe it was because he wanted to believe her, but he didn't think this girl could possibly have conducted forbidden rites to make herself immune to iron if she was a fae.

"Can I...let go now?" Brigid peered up at him.

"Uh, yes. Of course." Munch snatched the iron rod back and stuffed it into his quiver.

Brigid held up her palm, as if for his inspection. "See, I'm not burned. I'm not a fae."

Was that a glint of his spit on her palm? Before he could get a good look beyond noting that her palm was, indeed, unburned, she lowered her hand and smoothed it over her skirt as if to subtly swipe it clean.

He turned away to hide his wince. Here was the prettiest girl he'd ever met, and all she'd remember about him was that he had drooled. So smooth.

"Sorry I didn't believe you. I'm a forester. I need to be careful." Munch unstrung his bow and slid it into its place strapped across his back.

Maybe the fact that he was a forester would help improve his image in her mind. Perhaps if he reminded her that he was a forester often enough on the walk to the castle, she'd start to see him as a handsome and capable adult, not a bumbling boy.

Right. And maybe the fae had a potion that could erase the last few minutes from her mind before he died from embarrassment.

"Understandable." Brigid halted next to his elbow. She was smiling, but something in her stance remained tense. "So, are you going to take me to Robin and Guy?"

He'd been so focused on trying to determine if she was a threat that he hadn't considered this from her perspective. Here she was, alone with a strange young man in the middle of the forest.

And he hadn't even been polite enough to tell her his name yet.

He gestured back the way he'd come. "Yes, I'll take you to them. I'm Munch, by the way. Robin is my older sister."

That seemed to relax the tense set of Brigid's shoulder. She fell into step behind him as he led the way along the faint trail through the Greenwood. It wasn't much of a trail. Just a slightly more open spot through the forest, and only a forester or a trained tracker would notice the way the leaves were faintly disturbed.

They strolled in silence for a few minutes before Brigid's voice came from behind him. "So...Munch, huh?"

He released a long sigh. "It's a nickname. My full name is Mungoe."

She made a smothered sound somewhere between a snort and a giggle. "I'm sorry, I shouldn't laugh. It's rude."

"No, it's all right. I'm used to it." Munch shrugged his shoulders. He couldn't bring himself to glance over his shoulder to see the look on her face. "It's a—"

"Name from an old legend, I know. I grew up near a

village on the far side of the Greenwood, after all. I know the story."

That blasted story. If only his mother hadn't loved it so much that she'd named him after the main character. There were some names that worked better in stories than they did in real life.

"My mother loved the legends." Munch gave another shrug, hunching his shoulders underneath the straps for his bow. "And after my five older brothers, she and my father were running out of boys' names. So I ended up as Mungoe."

"At least they are fun legends." Brigid's footsteps crunched closer until she appeared next to him. Here, the forest was clear enough that they could walk side-by-side.

The legends of Sir Mungoe were good stories, and if it hadn't been for his name, Munch would have enjoyed sitting around the fire listening to them.

Instead, he'd grown up listening to Alan spout the story, only to have all his older siblings turn to him and tease him about the epic heroics the Mungoe of the story could accomplish. That Mungoe could walk for days carrying impossible amounts of gear without ever needing to eat or sleep. That Mungoe could take out fifty enemies without getting a single scratch. That Mungoe could leap mountains. Literally, the guy jumped over an entire mountain range in one of the legends.

But Munch was just...Munch. He could never measure up to the stories.

"I guess." Munch tried, but he couldn't feign enthusiasm for either his name or the Mungoe legends.

Brigid lapsed into silence for a few strides before she

glanced at him. "I'm named after someone from legends as well."

"Oh, right. There are legends about a Brigid, aren't there?" Munch couldn't remember any details about them. The stories didn't have nearly enough fighting to satisfy his family's tastes in stories. Fictional characters jumping over mountains and slaying villains was more their thing.

"Yes. She's pretty cool. She's known for being exceptionally clever and doing many impossible things." Brigid ducked around a tree branch.

"Do you ever feel burdened by having to live up to a legend?" Munch sneaked a peek at Brigid as she swerved around a tree growing next to the path.

She flashed him a grin, and it lit her face so that she was even prettier than before. "No, not really. The stories inspire me to be just as great. Perhaps I can't do all the fantastical things the Brigid of legends did, but I can still live my life in a way that makes it worthy of legends."

"Yes." Munch glanced at her again and decided to risk sounding boastful by saying his next thought. "I'm already in a few legends, actually. You wouldn't have heard of them, since they became popular after your family left for the Fae Realm."

If he was remembering what Meg had told them when she had visited. While it had been two years' time for them in the Fae Realm, it had been nearly five years here in the Human Realm. The legends about the Hood and his merry band of outlaws hadn't really started spreading until around then, and the stories hadn't truly taken off until the past few months when Alan had started singing ballads he'd written to entertain the visiting nobility at Gysborn.

"There were a few rumors about an outlaw of the

Greenwood floating around the village before we left." Brigid looked away from him, her expression falling as the light went out of her eyes. "I remember thinking how nice it would have been if a dashing outlaw saved us from Cullen before he carted us away to sell us as indentured servants."

Meg had told them about the death and danger the drought had brought on their family, causing them to leave the Human Realm entirely. But it was different, somehow, hearing about it from Brigid.

Munch let the crunching of their feet fill the silence between them for several moments. What could he say to something like that? Sure, he'd been in danger as an outlaw and he'd lost his parents like Brigid had, but he'd always had his family. He'd always felt safe, even as an outlaw. "I'm sorry we weren't able to help your village. We did what we could."

"I know, and I'm not trying to make you feel guilty or anything." Brigid's smile returned just as quickly as it had fled. "It all worked out, in the end. My family is very happy in the Fae Realm, and I can't imagine life anywhere else."

"I'm glad you found a place where you are happy." Munch hurried forward and held a branch out of Brigid's way.

The smile she gave him nearly had him walking straight into a tree. He caught himself at the last minute and covered the ungraceful dodge by giving the tree a pat, as if the tree was a particular favorite of his or something. It was a beech. A rather nice, large beech. A good tree.

Yet when he glanced at Brigid again, her mouth pressed into a tight line that couldn't hide the way her grin was attempting to break free.

Great. He couldn't help but keep embarrassing himself with her.

He could only hope that when they reached the castle, Robin would be on her best behavior. The last thing he needed was his sister adding to his embarrassment.

Chapter Three

Brigid found herself sneaking glances at the young man beside her as they hiked through the Greenwood. His brown hair was a little shaggy, falling across his forehead and into his eyes, which were a deep brown that sent tingles down her spine every time she met them. The faintest hint of a light brown fuzz dotted his chin and his upper lip. He was taller than her and lean. His shoulders didn't look broad enough for the bow he carried while a sword and a quiver of arrows hung from the belt slung around his hips.

And his smile…that lopsided smile was the cutest thing about him. When he wasn't drooling around the iron he'd clamped in his teeth, that was.

She shook herself. Focus. She was a capable young woman with more sense than this. She wasn't here to moon over a cute boy. She was here to learn how to fight the fae from the foresters of the Greenwood.

Well, *he* was a forester of the Greenwood. Would Lady

Robin assign Munch to teach Brigid what she needed to know?

A squeezing filled Brigid's chest and climbed up into her throat at the thought. Did she want him to be her teacher? Or was she dreading it? Perhaps both.

A brightness shone ahead of them, and soon Brigid could make out a road and fields beyond the edge of the forest. Their hike was almost over. Her feet were thankful, but the rest of her would have gladly prolonged this tramp through the forest. After that interesting start to their meeting, the walk had turned out to be surprisingly pleasant. It had been a long time since she'd been able to stroll through the woods with a good-looking boy.

Come to think of it, had she ever done something like this? Sure, there had been that one time when she'd been fourteen when she'd gone on a stroll with William Robert Moody during those few short months when the drought had abated and the whole village had turned out to celebrate.

The celebration had been premature. The drought had come back shortly afterwards even worse than ever. And William Robert had talked about his pet toad the entire time, and she'd been thankful he hadn't even attempted to kiss her. It would have been awkward kissing a boy when all she could think about was if he'd washed his hands since he'd held his pet last.

She would always remember that as the last night she'd been carefree for a long, long time. Shortly afterwards, her father had been taken away by Cullen, to die only a few months after that. Their mother had died soon after they received word of his death.

Brigid gave herself another good shake as she and

Munch stepped from the forest and onto the gravel road extending from the village along the river to the castle perched on the hill above.

The castle on the hill was a fortress with thick stone walls, intimidating round towers at each of the corners, and flat, battlemented parapets at the tops rather than the more decorative turrets.

For a moment, Brigid's steps slowed as she took it in. How much she had changed in the past two years. As a simple farmgirl, she hadn't known how to read or write. She would have been quaking in her homespun dress as she padded on bare feet toward a duke's castle.

Now, she was dressed in fabrics fine enough to be worn by nobility. Her boots were sturdy and knee-high, such an excess of leather that she never could have afforded before. She spent her days casually speaking with Queen Hippolyta and King Theseus. She could read and write, and a part of her suspected the magic of the Fae Realm had made it easier to learn.

Munch scratched at the back of his neck and glanced at her. "Before we get to the castle, I thought...well..."

Her heart beat harder in her chest, and she clasped her hands in front of her. What was he going to say? Was he going to ask if they could walk in the forest again? Did he feel the same attraction to her that she felt to him?

"I need to warn you about my family," he said in a whoosh of breath.

Oh. Not at all what she was expecting. She covered her disappointment with a smile. After all, why should she be disappointed? She'd only known Munch for a few hours. Sure, they'd bonded on this hike. But that was it. "My sister and brother-in-law said they enjoyed the meal they shared with your family. It was fun."

"Fun would be one thing to call it." Munch grimaced, his shoulders hunching. "They can be a bit *much* at times."

"I live in a magic House that dumps you in the wash grotto if it thinks you are too dirty and with a talking pony companion who dispenses life advice. I think I can handle whatever your family can dish out." Brigid found herself giving Munch an especially flirtatious grin. What was wrong with her? She'd just met him. She needed to get a grip.

But she was eighteen, he was a cute young man, and there was just no talking sense to the part of herself that was attracted to him.

"Ah, well, then maybe my family won't seem so strange." Munch smiled right back at her, and it did something funny to her stomach.

Ugh. They needed to get to his family's castle before she totally fell head over heels in puppy love.

Even if the puppy love gave her a bright, fizzing feeling that was rather nice. Like the feeling she got when trying on a pretty dress, but better.

At the castle gate, Munch announced them to the guards, then the guards pulled one of the gates open enough for them to step inside.

The walls hemmed in a cobblestone courtyard before the square keep that dominated the center of the castle. The main doors to the keep were flung open, and servants and guards alike strode back and forth, loading a wagon with something gold and glittering.

A tall woman dressed in a leather tunic and green trousers stood next to a thick-muscled man in a leather apron. The woman had a bow on her back and a quiver at her hip much like Munch did, and her long hair was a touch more gold than Brigid's. She gestured from the wagon to the man next to her as she spoke. "Now remember, you're to use part of this to make the new fixtures for the castle first. Any extra you can make to sell."

"Thank you, Your Grace." The man bowed, sweeping the wagon with a calculating eye. "I think there will be quite the market for items made from faerie gold. It glitters like real gold, but isn't as expensive."

"For now, at least. If it becomes too popular, the prices might go up." Robin tapped her sword's hilt. "Reinhault left us with quite the bounty of faerie gold in the vaults, but it isn't an endless supply."

"We'll make the most of it while it lasts, Your Grace. Never fear." The man—the village blacksmith, if Brigid were to guess—tipped his head to her in a mix between a bow and a salute. He moved off to help secure the load.

Robin turned to them, grinned, then sauntered across the courtyard to join them. "Munch. I thought you were on a patrol of the Greenwood. Don't tell me you tripped over a pretty maiden while you were at it?"

"Kinda, yeah." A red flush crept up Munch's face, and he scratched at the back of his neck, not looking at Brigid.

Brigid swept into a small curtsy. "Lady Robin, I'm Brigid of the Court of Knowledge. Meg is my older sister."

"Meg! Yes, she's a hoot. Did she and her family get home all right?" Robin waved in the direction of the Greenwood.

"Yes. They arrived home last night." Brigid straightened out of her curtsy and took in Robin's relaxed, confident stance. There was something about the way she rested a hand on her sword's hilt that spoke of skill. Queen

Hippolyta would likely make Robin a member of the Court of Swordmaidens on the spot if they ever met in person. "Is there somewhere more private where we could talk? Meg mentioned you might be willing to help me with a mission I'm on."

Robin's eyes danced with a gleam as she nodded. "Of course. Guy is in his study. We can go there. Munch, lunch will be served in the dining hall shortly. Can you see that a tray is brought to the study?"

"Of course." Munch nodded, then he sent a last, lingering glance at Brigid as if he was reluctant to leave.

And she was reluctant to watch him go. Sure, she had come all this way to speak with Robin and Guy, and she wasn't sure how much she should say in front of anyone else.

But as Munch strode away, she felt strangely small and alone.

"Follow me." Robin spun on her heel and led the way into the castle's keep.

Inside, worn green rugs lined the center of the corridors while the brass candelabras were tarnished and a few were broken. The cheap tallow candles dripped onto the floor in a way Brigid recognized. Her family, too, had used tallow instead of beeswax, though they had to use the candles as sparingly as possible because even tallow candles were too expensive.

Brigid followed Robin up a set of stairs and down another corridor before Robin flung open a door without bothering to knock.

"Robin," the black-haired man growled without even looking up from where he sat glowering at a stack of paperwork on his desk.

"I see I'm rescuing you from your paperwork just in time, if you've resorted to that glower and tone of voice." Robin sauntered across the room before she perched on the corner of Duke Guy's desk.

"I'm using that tone of voice because you didn't knock. Yet again." Guy swung his glower up to Robin, his mouth turned severely downward where it was framed by his short beard and mustache.

Brigid hovered in the doorway. Should she just duck away and come back later? She didn't want to get in the middle of an argument between husband and wife, and Duke Guy's voice and expression were downright scary.

"I never knock. If I knocked, you'd stab me for being a fae in disguise." Robin reached, as if she was going to flick his ear.

Duke Guy caught her hand, then pressed a kiss to the back of her knuckles. "Too true." A hint of a smile broke through his glower. "I'm glad of the rescue from my paperwork, milady."

Oh. They'd been joking. Brigid had *not* been able to tell, and she was usually good at reading people. But Duke Guy was just so dismally stern. He could give Lord Chauvlyn a lesson in cheerlessness. Such an odd contrast against his boisterously cheerful wife.

"Always happy to provide a little adventure in your life." Robin swiveled on the desk so that she was facing Brigid instead of Duke Guy. "This is Brigid. She is Meg's younger sister, and she's come to talk with us about a mission of some kind. Sounds like fun, so of course we're going to help her with whatever it is."

Duke Guy sighed and eyed Robin again. "We haven't even heard what she has to say yet." He shot a glance at

Brigid. "Not that I doubt its importance. I merely wish to hear all the details before I agree to anything. Especially when it involves the fae."

"I suppose that is a wise precaution. I have no wish to start another years-long drought." Robin leaned back on her hands and faced Brigid. "All right. Come in, close the door, and tell us all about it."

Brigid did just that, then sank into one of the chairs in front of the desk. She drew in a deep breath, smoothed her skirt, and faced the duke and duchess. "I'm putting together a league to help me to rescue humans who have been captured by the fae. I have allies in the Fae Realm who will help me there, but I'll need allies here in the Human Realm to alert me if there are rumors of stolen humans. You could also provide a place where I can safely take the rescued humans so that they can be returned to their homes. It may not always be possible for me to return them to their correct kingdom or place in the world."

"This is a dangerous mission of yours." Duke Guy steepled his fingers and regarded Brigid. "The fae will not like having their captives snatched from them."

"It sounds gloriously dangerous." Robin swung her long legs, her grin widening. "Of course we'll help."

"Robin." Duke Guy dragged out her name.

"What?" Robin glanced over her shoulder at him. "Don't tell me that you're going to refuse?"

"No." Duke Guy heaved a darkly grim sigh. "I would just like a moment to properly consider before we leap headfirst into this danger."

"Where's the fun in looking before leaping?" Robin smirked at him. "Besides, what is there to consider? We're foresters. We already fight the fae when they make the mistake of stepping into our forest. And this is your chance to strike back at the fae who held you captive for so long by rescuing others they've taken captive."

Guy's mouth pressed into a tight line, but he gave a grim nod. "You are correct."

"As always," Robin added.

"Not *as always*." Duke Guy poked her waist, making her squirm. "You have been wrong about plenty of things, Hood. Such as thinking that turning outlaw is a proper way to deal with society's problems."

"I suppose I *may* have been wrong in that case." Robin leaned farther back so that she could press a kiss to Duke Guy's cheek.

Brigid shifted and glanced toward the door. Perhaps she should sneak away and come back later? Maybe when Munch brought up the dinner tray?

Robin straightened and faced Brigid again. "All right, we're in."

"But let's discuss the details of how you plan to make this feasible." Duke Guy shot a glance at Robin. "Even you have to agree that something like this needs a proper plan in place."

"Oh, of course." Robin rested her hands on her knees to study Brigid. "Tell us. What do you have so far?"

Brigid slumped against the back of her chair and found herself talking over her plans with these two. Robin might be wild enough to put the fae to shame, and Duke Guy appeared the grim villain, but the two of them had minds as sharp as a manticore's teeth.

A knock sounded on the door before Munch's voice came through the oak. "I brought food."

"See, *he* knocks," Duke Guy muttered under his breath.

"I'm not sure where he got his manners since he clearly didn't get them from me." Robin grinned before she raised her voice. "Come in, Munch."

He opened the door, juggling a large tray in his other hand.

Brigid leapt to her feet to help, but he was already hurrying inside, tray in hand. All she succeeded in doing was in getting in his way. She dodged to the left at the same time he did. Then when she tried to go right, he was also going right. "Sorry." She halted with an embarrassed laugh.

Munch halted as well and, for a moment, they just blinked at each other. Then he cleared his throat. "I'll go left."

She waited until he moved before she stepped farther out of his way.

While Munch set the tray on the desk, Brigid took her seat once again, smoothing her skirts to give her hands something to do.

Robin leaned across the desk and snagged a bowl of stew and slice of bread. "The only question now, Brigid, is how do you feel about early mornings?"

"And before you answer, know that when Robin says early, she means *early*." Duke Guy's tone dropped into dour as he claimed his own stew and slice of bread.

"Really, *really* early." Munch dropped into the chair next to Brigid. He started to reach for a bowl, halted, then glanced at Brigid. He leaned back, gesturing for her to pick her bowl before him.

That flutter was back in her stomach. Such a chivalrous gesture. She grabbed a bowl, not really looking at the contents, as her cheeks heated a bit.

"I..." What were they talking about again? Oh, right. Early mornings. "I'm fine with them, I think?"

"Good. Because you'll start your training with me bright and early tomorrow morning." Robin dipped her bread into her stew before she stuffed a large bite into her mouth.

Munch took the last bowl and glanced between Robin and Brigid. "Training for what?"

Robin shrugged and waved at Brigid. "It's up to you how much we tell him. Though, we'll have to tell my brothers something. They're going to help with this plan of yours."

How much should she tell Munch? He was a forester, just like Robin. Surely he had the training to protect himself, even if the fae should question him about the Primrose, the alter-ego she was forming for herself.

But sudden, strange nerves twisted her stomach at the thought of telling Munch. What would he think of her, once he knew what she was planning?

Why was she nervous? It wasn't like she was planning anything wrong or scandalous. She was going to be a hero to the humans, even if she'd have to hide her true identity from most.

Brigid swallowed and drew in a deep breath. "There's this...League forming in the Fae Realm, led by the Primrose. We're going to rescue humans who have been captured by the fae."

"And you're going to help the Primrose? That sounds really cool." Munch leaned forward, meeting her gaze with those deep brown eyes of his.

"Not exactly." Her stomach twisted even worse.

"Oh, you're going to be a messenger girl. That's why you need Robin's training. She'll teach you how to travel the faerie circles." Munch nodded, as if that made perfect sense to him.

Brigid looked away from Munch and caught the pitying eyebrow that Robin was giving her.

It was silly, but Munch's assumptions hurt. Sure, they'd only known each other for a few hours. And Brigid didn't look like a tough, swashbuckling girl like his older sister Robin. Of course he'd assume a girl who loved dresses and didn't carry a weapon would be a mere messenger girl instead of the leader of the League.

Perhaps she should correct Munch.

But she found herself mumbling, "Yes, I'm the messenger girl." She popped a bite of soup into her mouth, ignoring the burn of the hot liquid against her tongue that competed with the burn of tears in her eyes.

It wasn't like she'd come here to flirt with a handsome boy. She was here for allies and for training. That was it.

Chapter Four

Brigid's heart pounded harder as she faced the faerie circle with the rather crazy Lady Robin.

Robin grinned and paced at the edge of the ring of spruces that marked this particular faerie circle. "We foresters use the circles to move quickly around the Greenwood. We call it walking the faerie paths. When you know how to walk the faerie paths, you can control where and even when you exit."

"When?" Brigid glanced from Robin to the faerie circle.

"Yes, though it can be tricky. I usually only lose an hour or two when I skirt the edge of a circle." Robin shrugged. "Family lore has it that some foresters could even walk back in time if they got good enough at it."

"That's impressive." Brigid couldn't imagine having that much control when walking through a faerie circle. Every time she had gone through, she hadn't been able to breathe, much less think. How was she going to master the art of actually walking the faerie paths instead of simply stepping through a circle? "What about walking between the realms?"

"That's more complicated, for sure." Robin traced her fingers over one of the spruce boughs. "When I walk the faerie paths, I stick to the Human Realm side. Makes it easier not to lose time or get lost. Time gets a bit topsy-turvy where the realms meet. Even talking animal companions struggle to navigate the swirling way the realms interact."

"Is there anything I can do to make it easier?" Even with Buddy's help, Basil and Meg had lost eight months when they returned for the rest of the family. And that had actually been on the better end of things. If Brigid was doing this on her own, how long would it take for her to return those who had been kidnapped to their homes? Worse, what if hundreds of years passed and she didn't even have Robin, Duke Guy, and the foresters to help in the Human Realm?

Robin pulled an iron rod from the quiver at her waist and brandished it. "We foresters carry iron rods. Gripping them helps counter the magic and prevents the Fae Realm from luring us in deeper. For you, though, the Fae Realm already has you. An iron rod would probably be a good idea, but the lure you'll have to fight is from the Human Realm trying to take you back. You'll want to take something from the Fae Realm with you to keep you grounded there."

Huh. Brigid hadn't thought of that, but it made sense, in a weird way.

And she knew exactly what she was going to take with her.

Robin held out a second iron rod. "Ready to practice walking the faerie path?"

Brigid took the iron rod and forced herself to smile with that same reckless tilt as Robin. "Yes."

If she was going to survive this mission of hers, then she would have to learn to take on a bit of Robin's recklessness.

Reckless. Perhaps she would need to develop her own signature laugh. But instead of Robin's swashbuckling confidence, perhaps a persona of inanity. The more empty-headed she appeared, the more underestimated she would be. If the rumors built this image of a dashing, fae male hero, then those seeking her would never look twice at an empty-headed girl who could clearly never pull off what she was going to attempt as the Primrose.

Robin stepped into the faerie circle, and Brigid followed right on her heels, gripping the iron rod the duchess had given her tightly.

The dizzying pressure of magic closed around her as it usually did, but it didn't overwhelm as much.

Brigid drew in a steadying breath. The air here smelled like a mix of the rich, earthy forest of the Human Realm and the thickly floral scent that clung to the Fae Realm.

Robin's eyes held an almost wild light as she smirked at Brigid. "I always love this part, standing on the precipice of adventure. Here on the faerie paths, anything is possible."

It did feel like that, didn't it? As if she could tumble off this strange path she walked and find herself in an adventure straight out of one of Basil's storybooks.

They stood on a tiny patch of green surrounded by haze. Through the haze on one side, the trees of the Greenwood were a distant, indistinct shape. To the other side, the brighter green of the Fae Realm beckoned in a bright splash of color.

"I can't really teach you the next part." Robin gestured with her iron rod at the haze around them. "Walking the faerie paths is a matter of instinct as much as training. You have to learn how to sense your way along the faerie paths."

"All right. So how do I sense my way?" Brigid glanced around, then halted when turning her head swirled the scene around them like she was stuck in a bowl of water being swirled by a giant.

"Close your eyes and sink into your senses." Robin closed her eyes as if to demonstrate. "Legend has it that my family had a fae ancestor who gifted us with a few handy instincts when it comes to magic. Do you have any fae ancestors, do you know?"

"Not that I know of. I'm fully human." Brigid closed her eyes and tried to sense what was around her. All she got was an overwhelming squeeze of magic. Nothing tugged at her or anything like that. She sighed and opened her eyes. "It's not working. I can sense the magic, but it is just...there. Everywhere."

"Hmm. That's going to be a problem." Robin opened her eyes, placed a hand on her hip, and studied Brigid. "But you're not so fully human anymore, are you? You've been living in the Fae Realm for the past two years. You're bound to a fae court. You're eating fae food and generally living like a fae. You might be fully human by blood, but you're fae by choice."

Brigid had never thought of it quite like that, but Robin had a point. "So what does that mean for traveling the realms?"

"Forget what I said about instincts. You don't have those. Not yet, anyway." Robin stepped closer and tapped Brigid's chest with her iron rod. "What you do have is a love for the Fae Realm."

"I don't..." Brigid paused. Did she love the Fae Realm?

Sure, it was her family's sanctuary. The haven which had rescued them from a lifetime of drudgery and slavery.

But her siblings loved the Fae Realm far more. Meg loved Basil, and both the House and the Great Library responded to her like they responded to few even among the fae. Viola and Sebastian had found their lifelong passion to work as librarians. Even Beatrice, despite her feud with Benedict, adored the Great Library and especially the bookwyrms.

What did Brigid love about the Fae Realm? She was there because her family was there, and because she wanted to rescue those who had been snatched by the fae. The realm itself wasn't particularly special to her, was it?

If it was up to her, would she choose to return to the Human Realm? Leave everything and everyone behind and settle down in a nice, normal village like Gysborn. Perhaps she would settle down with a nice, normal young man like Munch and have a nice, normal life.

If she stayed in the Fae Realm, she would give up everything normal. She would be fighting alone, the head of her League. Instead of marriage and safety, she would have danger and adventure and all things she didn't crave the way Robin did.

The safe, normal life of the Human Realm was far more tempting than she would like to admit, but…

Her family. Buddy. The House. The Great Library. Queen Hippolyta and her swordmaidens. King Theseus. Head Librarian Marco. All of the librarians she'd come to know. Brigid couldn't leave them. She loved them.

And she loved the realm. Its intense colors and almost gaudy beauty. The way the realm's rules seemed made to be broken.

She was a fae by choice. She had chosen the Fae Realm as her own, and that made it special to her in a way that even those who had been born there didn't understand.

As she had the thought, something red sprang up in the patch of moss at their feet.

Brigid knelt and touched its petals. A wild fae primrose. The wanderer's flower.

"A pimpernel?" Robin leaned over her shoulder to peer at it.

Even as Brigid watched, a line of primroses appeared, leading toward the bright green of the Fae Realm.

Leading her home.

"Not yet, I'm afraid," Brigid whispered as she touched the flower's delicate petals again. "I need to finish training here first."

A slight shiver twanged through the haze around them before more wild fae primroses appeared, this time stretching toward the Human Realm.

"There's your answer." Robin grinned and waved to the flowers. "That's how you navigate the faerie paths. Lead on. Let's see where we end up."

Brigid pushed to her feet and followed the path laid out by the primroses. After a few strides, she stepped through the shimmer and stumbled into the earthy emptiness of the Greenwood.

Robin strolled out of the faerie circle behind her, her hand on her hip again as she took in the forest around them. "Hmm. Not bad. We popped out of a faerie circle about an hour north of the circle where we went in, but that's far better than ending up on the other side of the world. Which could have happened, if you'd strayed off the path."

That had been a possibility? That would have been nice to know before Robin had told her to just wander wherever the flowers led. At least she hadn't led them that much astray.

"Now we just need to find out what day it is." Robin set out into the Greenwood, setting a brisk pace with her long legs.

Brigid trotted to keep up. Oh, right. Hopefully she hadn't lost too much time while dithering in the faerie circle.

Her breath caught. What if months had passed? Or years? What if she'd accidentally stolen Robin away from her family forever?

"Oh, stop worrying." Robin flapped her hand at her. "I sense that it hasn't been that long. I don't think more than a day has passed. I left word with Guy that I might not be back right away, so he won't be too worried. I don't think so, anyway. I wouldn't have let you take that particular path if I'd sensed anything was too amiss."

Well, that was…comforting. Sort of. Training with Robin was much more lackadaisical than practice with Queen Hippolyta.

As long as Brigid learned what she needed to know, the training methods didn't matter.

MUNCH STROLLED beside Brigid through the Greenwood, his heart pounding with each step.

After spending three weeks with them, Brigid was returning to the Fae Realm today. Sure, he would likely see her again, but he didn't know when. And this moment felt like one where he should say or do something important. What, he didn't know. But it needed to be memorable.

"I guess you're probably looking forward to seeing your family again." Munch kicked at a pine cone. Ugh. That was the best he could come up with? Of course she was looking forward to seeing her family again.

"Yes. Hopefully time hasn't passed too quickly over in the Fae Realm. I might have been gone only a day. Or maybe it has been six weeks over there. Who's to say?" Brigid shrugged, her gaze focused on the forest ahead of them. "I've been practicing, but I'm still learning how to navigate the realms without losing too much time."

"I'm sure you'll do great." Munch smiled at her, wishing he could think of something better to say than this stilted conversation.

"Thanks." She returned his smile, and it sent a funny twisting sensation into his chest.

"The Primrose will be glad to have a skilled messenger like you on his team." Munch found himself drifting closer to her, his steps slowing.

Her smile dropped, and she turned away from him. "I'm sure he will."

What had he said wrong? Wouldn't she want a compliment on her skills? Girls were baffling, and having a sister like Robin hadn't prepared him for understanding someone like Brigid.

The silence stretched between them for several long moments as Munch wracked his brain for something to say. He liked Brigid. He couldn't let her just leave without saying something.

But what could he say? She was going back to the Fae Realm. She had a mission for this Primrose to undertake.

And he belonged here in the Human Realm with his family. He couldn't imagine leaving his sister and brothers. Not only were they a family, but they had been a merry band of outlaws. They were foresters. There was something deep and lasting about the bonds he shared with them, even when they annoyed him.

"When...when do you think you'll be back?" Munch tried to keep his stride nonchalant to hide how badly he wanted the answer to this question.

"I don't know. I'm not sure when I'll—I mean, when the Primrose will..." Brigid shook her head, still not looking at him. "Who's to say, really? Especially with how time moves between the realms. Even if I'm sent back tomorrow, that might be months from now here in the Human Realm."

Right. Munch's stomach sank. With how time moved, would he age so fast that soon he would be in his thirties while Brigid was still a teen?

He might as well give up on this attraction here and now. Forget about the time he and Brigid had spent together the past few weeks.

Or he'd forget about these past few weeks once Brigid left. Until then, he was going to make the most of this last stroll through the woods.

Ahead, the faerie circle appeared as a bright spot among the tree trunks and vegetation. He only had a few more minutes.

"Brigid..." He halted, turning toward her.

She slowed, then stopped. For a moment she stared ahead at the faerie circle before she faced him with a smile that seemed more fake than real plastered on her face. "Don't make this harder than it is. These last few weeks have been nice. But I'm not...we can't..."

"I know." Munch stepped a little closer. His heart pounded so hard that his chest ached while his palms had gone so sweaty that he feared he'd leave smears on his trousers if he tried to wipe them dry. "Is a kiss goodbye all right?"

Brigid blinked at him, then tipped her head in a tiny nod.

BRIGID STOOD on her toes and leaned upward right as he leaned down, and they ended up bumping more than kissing right at first.

And then when they did kiss...were kisses supposed to be this sloppy? She stood there for a moment, her hands at her sides, her mind screaming that this was absolutely awkward.

Then she pulled away, stumbling back a step and resisting the urge to wipe her mouth on her sleeve. Well, that was gross. So much for a first kiss filled with romance and sparks.

Her face burned like it had been scoured with dragon fire, and she couldn't bring herself to look at Munch. She liked talking to him and walking through the woods with him and her heart gave a nice little lurch when she looked at him.

She'd even been thinking that she should tell him the truth about her role.

But that kiss had been awful. And she just couldn't face him.

Spinning on her heel, she dashed for the faerie circle and all but threw herself into it, leaving Munch and that awkward kiss behind.

Oh, well. At least that kiss would make it easier to put Munch and the attraction she'd felt for him out of her mind. She needed to focus on her mission as the Primrose. That role left no room for romance and handsome boys with lopsided smiles and deep brown eyes.

MUNCH SAGGED against a tree and grimaced.

Were kisses supposed to be that...underwhelming? Based on the way Guy and Robin were always kissing, he'd been under the impression that kissing was a pleasant experience.

He must have done something wrong, though he wasn't sure what.

He'd blown it with Brigid. Maybe now he could put her out of his mind and focus on becoming a full-fledged forester now that he was eighteen. Nearly nineteen.

A summer romance. That was all this had been.

Too Many Chauvlyns

Note: This story takes place nearly two years after the events of *Forest of Scarlet (Court of Midsummer Mayhem Book One)* and contains spoilers for that book.

Chapter One

Brigid dragged herself through the Anywhere Door into the white marble hall, feet aching, exhaustion pressing deeply into her eyes.

At her side, Munch reached out and placed an arm around her waist, subtly steadying her.

Another human taken by the fae. Another successful rescue. Another jaunt through the faerie paths.

Brigid leaned into Munch, closing her eyes. Perhaps she would just fall asleep standing up, trusting that Munch would steer her back through the Anywhere Door that would take them to their House.

"Librarian Brigid? Forester Mungoe?"

Brigid sighed and peeled her eyes open, though she remained slumped against Munch. "Yes?"

Philostrate, steward for King Theseus, stood there, properly turned out even at this hour of the morning. "I apologize for taking you away from your rest, but King Theseus would like to speak with both of you."

Brigid muffled her groan against Munch's shoulder. If

King Theseus had only wanted their report—now that he was no longer hiding the fact that he was aiding the Wild Fae Primrose, he expected regular reports—he would wait until they were rested. This had to be important.

"Lead the way." Munch's arm tightened around Brigid, keeping her upright as he set off after Philostrate.

Brigid let her eyes fall closed, resting her eyes while she walked. The doors at the end of the hall opened and shut, then their footsteps were muffled against the carpet runner down the hallway of King Theseus's palace.

Another door opened, then Philostrate announced, "Librarian Brigid, Forester Mungoe, as you requested, my king."

Brigid cracked her eyes open and straightened so that she walked into the study on her own power.

King Theseus sat behind his desk, stacks of paperwork spread before him. He halted what he was doing and glanced up at their entrance.

Brigid dipped into an attempt at a curtsy before she collapsed into one of the chairs across from the king's desk. It was a good thing that King Theseus wasn't as stuffy or huffy as most fae kings, or he'd probably order her head chopped off for her affront in not waiting to be invited to sit.

Munch bowed, though he remained standing, taking up a place behind Brigid's chair in a way that suggested he didn't intend to sit.

"Brigid, Munch, thank you for coming. I take it your last mission went well?" King Theseus's tone remained level yet officious.

"Yes, though you'll forgive me if I wait to submit a more official report after I've slept." Brigid slouched deeper into the chair. She might just fall asleep right here. The leather chair wasn't all that comfortably plush, but it would do.

King Theseus waved the comment away. "If you think you can put off sleep for a little longer, I have a group of fae waiting in my blue reception room. They wish to speak with the Primrose, but I told them I couldn't promise anything."

Brigid pushed upright, the sleepiness banished at the tantalizing allure of a new mission. "Is it a trap? Who are they?"

"I questioned them extensively, and I don't think it is a trap." King Theseus leaned back in his chair, something in his dark eyes sad beneath his black eyebrows. "They are a group of pixies. According to them, a group of humans raided the Court of Dreams and stole nearly a dozen pixie babies from one of their flower nurseries. Queen Mab has done nothing to get them back. Desperate, the pixies have come here, hoping the Wild Fae Primrose will help them, even though they are fae."

Brigid clenched her fists, her nails biting into her palms. So far, she had concentrated her efforts on rescuing humans from the fae.

But it was just as awful when humans kidnapped fae. Fae *children.*

Munch's fingers tightened on the back of the chair, his knuckles turning white. "I remember hearing rumors about pirates in one of the southern kingdoms trafficking in pixies. I didn't pay attention at the time, and I didn't put a lot of credence on the gossip."

"But of all the fae, the pixies and the goblins would be the easiest for humans to prey on." Brigid's head spun, already working through the logistics and plans.

Munch's brother Alan was currently travelling through the southern kingdoms. If they could get a message to him, he might be able to track down the missing pixie children.

"We'll meet with them. Munch?" Brigid swiveled in her chair. "I think it is time for you to reprise your role as the silent and mysterious Primrose."

Munch nodded, then fished in one of the magical pockets of his tunic. He'd taken to wearing fae-made tunics since having magical pockets was so convenient.

He drew out a long, green cloak, which he swept over his shoulders. Digging into his pocket, he produced a combination kerchief and mask, and he tied it over his head so that most of his face was covered, along with his hair and his ears. Once that was done, he flipped the hood of his cloak over his head, shadowing his whole face.

Brigid, too, dug into a pocket and pulled out a mask of her own, though hers was a more decorative mask, like the one used for a masquerade ball.

Once she had her mask on, she nodded, first to King Theseus, then to the fae steward. "With your permission, King Theseus, please lead the way, Philostrate."

King Theseus gave his own nod and a wave of dismissal.

Philostrate clicked his heels, bowed, then motioned for Munch and Brigid to follow him.

Brigid mustered her strength, pushed to her feet, then followed Philostrate, Munch keeping pace.

The blue reception room was located only a few doors down the hallway from the study. Philostrate opened the door, then stood aside, announcing to the room, "The Wild Fae Primrose and his assistant."

Brigid strolled in first, plastered a soft smile on her face. Munch followed her, then took up a position next to the door against the wall, working the whole brooding and mysterious hero thing to the fullest.

As soon as she and Munch entered, the pixies stood, facing them with clasped hands and expectant faces that were almost too much to bear, knowing that she might not be able to help at all, if they couldn't locate the stolen children.

TRANSFORMED TO THEIR FULL-SIZED VERSION, the pixies stood half a foot or more shorter than Brigid. One had hair a cerulean blue while the other's was shocking pink. Their gossamer wings fluttered at their agitation while their flower petal or leaf outfits swathed them with surprising modesty for the Fae Realm.

Brigid forced herself to smile. Not a cheerful smile, but one of kindness and loss and comfort. She gestured over her shoulder at Munch. "The Primrose has agreed to hear your plea. What happened?"

The pixie with the blue hair stepped forward, glancing between Munch and Brigid before focusing on Brigid. "Pixie children are born small and vulnerable, and they are kept in communal flower nurseries where they can be guarded together. A week ago, one of these nurseries was raided by a group of humans. They killed two of the pixie guardians and wounded a third before disappearing through the faerie circle. We appealed to our queen, but she has refused to aid us."

There was so much pain in the pixie's voice that Brigid had to swallow a lump in her own throat. Perhaps it was foolish, but there wasn't a doubt in her mind that these pixies were telling the truth.

The pixie woman blinked, then focused on Munch with liquid turquoise eyes. "You are our only hope to see our children again. We can't venture into the Human Realm ourselves. But you have contacts in that realm. You have mercy on the kidnapped and vulnerable. I know you normally help humans, but please help us."

How could she refuse? These pixie children were in just as dire straits as the human children she usually rescued.

Brigid glanced over her shoulder at Munch, even though she had already made of her mind. With the hood and the mask, she couldn't make out the expression on his face or the look in his eyes. But he gave her a slight nod, letting her know that he would support her no matter the decision she made.

To the pixies, it would look like she had been consulting with the Primrose. They couldn't know that she *was* the Primrose, and her decision had already been made.

Brigid turned back to the two pixie women. "Of course the Primrose will help you. He aids the vulnerable, whether they are human or fae."

"Thank you." The pixie woman clasped her hands, her knees wobbling as if she was about to fall to her knees in gratitude. Behind her, the pink-haired one, who had remained silent, pressed her hands over her mouth as tears spilled down her glitter-dusted cheeks.

This was why Brigid had created the Primrose. To ease the pain of families who had lost loved ones to the evils of those who would steal and use others for their own gain.

Chapter Two

Brigid crouched in the undergrowth, peering past the thick foliage to the river mouth where a ship load of human pirates were lolling about on the beach, drinking, gambling, and boisterously celebrating.

"The pixie babies were on the ship, according to our acquaintance." Alan pointed at the ship, his movements low and slow so that it wouldn't draw attention if any of the pirates happened to look their way.

Brigid nodded, taking in the position of the ship where it was anchored in the river mouth, the setting sun setting the sails aflame in orange. There was no dock here, and the pirates had rowed smaller boats from the ship to the beach. Likely a few pirates had remained on board, but she couldn't see any movement on the decks at the moment.

Whoever sneaked on board would need to either steal one of the boats or swim. Both options had advantages and disadvantages.

"What's the plan?" Beside her, Munch fingered the fletchings of his arrows in the quiver at his belt.

"How long until the authorities arrive, do you think?" Brigid glanced from Munch to Alan.

Alan shrugged, his mouth pressing into a tight line. "It could be any minute. Or it could be hours yet. Sophie will do her best to convince them that there really are pirates in the area, but they might not listen to her."

They'd sent Sophie, Alan's wife, with their son bundled in a carrier on her back, to alert the authorities to the pirates.

It would have been rather convenient to let the local naval authorities swoop in and deal with the pirates. It would be risky to try to rescue the pixie children under the cloak of the confusion, but no less risky than doing it without such a distraction.

While Sophie could sound like a local, her dusky skin and dark eyes spoke of her heritage as one of the wandering peoples who preferred the traveling life across the kingdoms, which was how Alan met her. The wanderers were held in low regard by most in authority, if not actively run out of town. The authorities were just as likely to toss her out as listen to her.

"Then we can't base any plans on their timely arrival." It might be a bonus, but it wouldn't be a sure thing. Brigid studied the pirates again. That left only a few options. "Munch, you and I are going to sneak on the ship. Alan, you're going to distract the pirates. Hopefully they are too drunk to question what a minstrel is doing strolling this rather out of the way beach."

Alan grinned. "Won't be a problem. I can be rather convincing."

He eased deeper into the foliage before he took off his cloak, flipping it around so that the dark green was now on the inside, leaving a bright red, flashy material on the outside. He turned his cap inside out, revealing a yellow fabric. Fishing into his pocket, he pulled out a red feather and tucked it into the hat band. He picked up his lute, tipped his hat to them, and strode through the brush, heading for the beach.

Brigid glanced over the beach again. They'd have to swim. The pirates likely wouldn't be so distracted that they wouldn't notice a boat going missing. Nor could she be sure she and Munch could paddle quietly enough.

Sighing, she took off her cloak. It would just hamper her. "Ready for a swim."

Munch grimaced as he ditched his own cloak, then unbuckled his quiver. "I'll have to leave my bow and quiver behind. Too hard to keep dry."

"If this all goes well, then we won't need weapons." Brigid unlaced her boots, tugging them off one after the other.

"And if everything doesn't go well, as usually happens?" Munch pulled off his own boots.

"Then combat will be too close for bow and arrows anyway. Your sword will be better." Brigid assessed the rest of her clothing. There was nothing else she could ditch, unless she wanted to strip down to her underwear.

Munch was her husband, so there was nothing too scandalous there. But when it came to a choice between walking around in sopping wet clothing or fighting pirates in her underwear, she would rather stay dressed. Not to mention that the items in the magical pocket of her trousers might come in handy.

A clear tenor voice rang out into the early evening, accompanied by the strumming of a lute. As the voice drew closer, Brigid made out the words of a drinking song.

Some of the pirates around the fires reached for weapons. Others just raised their tankards and sloppily sang along.

The distraction had begun.

Brigid shared a look with Munch. Then Munch led the way through the brush, angling slightly upstream of the ship.

Smart. Brigid might be the planner, but Munch was the forester and ex-outlaw. He was the one to lead an infiltration like this.

At the edge of the river, Munch ducked behind a boulder that kept them out of sight of the pirates, should any of them glance upstream. He freed a large branch that had washed up on the bank in the eddy formed by the boulder.

He glanced over his shoulder, giving her a lopsided smile. "Perhaps a cliché, but it works."

"The classics always do." Brigid waded into the river, staying low and trying not to grimace too much at the river muck squishing between her toes. She was definitely not going to think about the turtles or leeches or other critters that might be lurking in the river mud. She preferred plans that involved pretty dresses and witty banter over ones that involved action and getting dirty. That was more Munch's thing.

Munch pushed the branch ahead of them, then sank into the river, holding the branch before them. He held his sword and daggers against the branch, out of sight but also out of the water. If any pirates looked their way, all they'd see would be a branch drifting on the current.

Brigid sank into the river up to her neck, scowling at the

cold water soaking through her clothes. The river was so choked with silt and mud that she couldn't see her hand only six inches beneath the surface as she swam. Who knew what fish and other critters were lurking, waiting to nibble on her toes. She would need a long soak in their bathing grotto in their House once this was all over.

Her skin crawled, and she banished the thoughts from her head. She couldn't let herself think about icky critters. All that mattered was rescuing the innocent pixie babies.

Munch steered them across the river, using the current to pull them along while skillfully maneuvering them so that no one watching would suspect the branch was being propelled.

As they neared the ship, Munch sent the branch on its way, then hugged the ship, navigating around the hull until they were on the far side of the ship from the pirates on the beach.

There, wooden boards had been nailed to the side of the ship, providing a crude ladder up the side. Earlier, the pirates had swarmed down it as easily as Brigid traipsed through an Anywhere Door.

Munch glanced over her shoulder at her, a question in his eyes.

Could she climb that? Brigid swallowed, then nodded. She'd have to.

Munch gestured for her to go first. She wasn't sure what he'd thought he'd do if she slipped and fell. He likely wouldn't be able to catch her.

She shook her head and pointed from him to the ladder. Better that he went first. If she fell, she'd just push off and land back in the water. She'd rather he went first and took out any pirate guards who might be waiting above.

Munch searched her face, then nodded. He gripped the first board, heaved himself out of the water with only the strength of his arms, then reached for the next board, hanging only from the grip of his fingers. He gathered himself, kicked with his legs, and lunged upward, grabbing hold of the next board. With another show of strength, he hauled himself upward until his feet were securely planted on the first board.

No way was Brigid going to manage that.

She swam below the board, kicked, and flung herself out of the water as high as she could. She grabbed the ledge with both hands, her fingers next to Munch's toes. She strained, but she couldn't lift herself out of the water, no matter how hard she kicked. She just didn't have the upper body strength for something like that.

Munch leaned over, then grabbed one of her wrists. He whispered, "On three."

She nodded, then focused on his face as he mouthed the countdown. On three, she kicked and strained to pull herself up with one hand. Munch heaved upward, balanced on his toes and his grip on a plank above him.

Together, they managed to get Brigid out of the water high enough that she could get a toe into the first of the boards. Once she was securely perched—or as secure as she could be—Munch let go of her wrist and climbed upward.

It was easier to get herself situated once Munch's feet and legs were out of the way. Climbing the plank ladder still wasn't easy. They were only two inches deep, and Brigid's fingers were slick with river water.

None of that seemed to bother Munch. He scurried up the side of the ship as easily as a squirrel would a tree.

Within seconds, he rolled onto the deck, disappearing out of her sight.

As Brigid continued her slow way upward, a few thumps came from above, followed by a muffled cry. It wasn't loud enough to carry far, barely audible even to Brigid. The noise of the singing—which had just gotten more raucous and raunchy, accompanied by Alan's lute and clear tenor—would have covered any noise they made.

When she finally reached the top, she rolled onto the deck, her arms quivering. She would have just laid there, panting, but a large blood spot was growing on the deck. A body lay a few feet away, dressed in the haphazard rags of a pirate.

Brigid would have felt worse that their mission was resulting in deaths but this was a pirate and this crew was responsible for stealing children. If she felt any pity, it was for Munch being forced to kill.

Munch was nowhere to be seen. Neither were any pirates.

Brigid got to her feet, still keeping low to stay below the tall ship's rail. She padded across the deck, coming across another body before she reached the door to what she guessed was the captain's cabin.

Before she could open the door, a figure stepped out of the shadows. She reached into her pocket, digging for the rapier she always kept there. Before she did so much as wrap her fingers around the hilt, she recognized Munch.

"I've searched the deck. We're clear." Something tight and dark twisted Munch's mouth in a way she had rarely seen on him. In other words, all the pirates on the deck were dead or incapacitated. "I haven't had a chance to search below decks yet."

"I doubt anyone will be lurking below. Why stay below when one can party on the beach?" Brigid rested a hand on the latch. "Besides, I don't think we'll need to go below. Unless I miss my guess, the captain will keep the stolen pixies close."

She pushed open the door and ducked inside. Even though she wasn't that tall, the low ceiling of the ship's cabin still felt too close.

A ship's bed, hung from the ceiling with ropes, was covered with rumbled, silk sheets. The table, desk, and wardrobe were all secured in place, but the jumble of elegant, expensive detritus wasn't secured, lumped onto the desk, table, and floor. An exotic, spicy scent filled the space, nearly choking in the evening warmth.

How were they going to find anything in here? Where would the captain keep a handful of pixie babies? They wouldn't take up much space in their walnut shell cradles. All eleven of them could fit one's cupped palms.

Brigid poked through the items on the desk while Munch used his sword to peer through the items in the pirate's wardrobe.

Nothing. Brigid spun in a slower circle. The floor likely wasn't an option. When she knelt and checked under the hanging bed, all she found was dust, grime, and a few unmentionable items. But no walnut shells or pixie children.

Where else a pirate stow his most valuable, stolen items? He had braved the Fae Realm for these children. He wouldn't put them in the hold or trust them out of his sight.

Her skin flushed cold. What if he had taken them with him to the beach? He could be carrying them around in a pocket of his coat, keeping them close, even now.

Would he do that? Or would he be too worried about his own crew picking his pockets?

They had to be here. Hopefully he would trust the security of his cabin more than he trusted his pockets around his light-fingered crew members.

She proceeded to tear the cabin apart with less care for the captain's belongings than before. Still nothing.

Munch pulled up the seats to the window bench. Then he froze. "Brigid."

She hurried to his side as he lifted a small, wooden box from the window seat. A large padlock held the lid shut.

Munch set the box on his lap, pulled out his picks, and had the padlock open within a few seconds. Sharing a glance with Brigid, Munch lifted the lid, revealing the contents.

Eight walnut shells lay on a padding of velvet.

Trying to keep her fingers from shaking, Brigid picked up the first shell and opened it.

A tiny baby, barely bigger than a kidney bean, curled on a miniature mattress made of moss with a flower petal for a blanket. Brigid had to stare at the baby for a long moment to make sure the baby was breathing.

She checked the rest of them, and they were all breathing, though listless. It couldn't have been good for them to be stuffed in this nearly airless box in this hot, stuffy cabin.

Only once she had determined that these eight were alive did Brigid meet Munch's gaze. "There are only eight here. Three are missing."

Munch's jaw worked, but his voice remained soft as he held his gaze. "We knew there was a possibility one or more had already been sold. The rumors of pirates with pixies for sale was how we tracked them. Stories like that don't get around unless the pirates were actively looking for buyers."

"I was still hoping…" Brigid swallowed, blinking. She was rescuing eight of the eleven. Pretty good odds. Yet it still felt like a failure because of those missing three.

"We'll find them." Munch rested his hand on hers, waiting until she met his gaze. "It might take a little longer, but we'll get there. Now let's get these little ones off this ship."

As much as she hated doing it, she closed the lid of the box. It was the safest way to transport the babies at this point. She couldn't place them in her magical pocket—living people or plants couldn't go in the magical pocket—and her regular pockets would probably jostle them.

Now to get them off the ship without harming them further.

As Munch helped her to her feet, a boom tore through the air. The crash of splintering wood tore through the ship below them even as the deck shook beneath her feet.

Munch's grip tightened on her. "I think the navy has arrived."

Plundering pirates, why now? Brigid couldn't even blame the bad timing on anyone other than herself. Calling in the navy was her plan, after all.

"Go." She gave Munch a shove. "You need to grab the captain in the chaos. We need to question him to find out who he sold the three pixie babies to."

"I can't leave you here." Munch hesitated, his grip still tight on her hand.

"I'll be fine. You took out all the guards, and there's nothing you can do to protect me from cannon balls if you stayed." Brigid tugged out of his grip, then hurried for the door, clutching the box to her. "I'll be right behind you. Now go."

With one last glance at her, Munch grabbed his sword, then rushed from the cabin.

Brigid followed on his heels, though she didn't run. She didn't dare shake the box too much, not when it held such precious cargo.

At the rail, Munch took a running leap and dove into the river, carving a smooth arc before landing with only a minimal splash.

At the mouth of the river, two naval gunboats rowed into place. They had some of the newfangled cannons fueled by gunpowder that was becoming more the thing in this part of the world.

The pirates on the beach were scattering, running for weapons, their ship, or the forest.

None of those options were good for Brigid. First she needed to get off this ship.

She made her way to the rail, taking in the wooden ladder built into the side of the ship that she'd used to get up here. How was she supposed to climb down using only one hand? She'd barely gotten up with two hands.

Another boom split the night. The cannonball splashed into the river with a sploosh, sending waves that shoved into the small jolly boats filled with pirates.

She didn't have a lot of time.

Digging into her magical pocket, she pulled out a shawl and a long sash that she used for one of her disguises. Opening the box, she took all the shells out, then tipped the box on its side. She layered the shawl inside, adding in the walnut cradles to keep them upright with the box on its side. Hopefully she wasn't smothering the babies. She'd take out the shawl as soon as she could.

Once the padding was in place, she closed the box and held it to her chest. It wasn't easy to wrap the sash around herself, tying the box securely to her chest.

With her hands now free, she eased her feet over the side of the ship, feeling with her toes until she found the first plank. Rung by rung, she lowered herself down, careful not to bump the box.

When her seeking toes touched water instead of the next rung, she eased into the water. Hanging onto the ship with one hand, she untied the box. Holding it above the water, she let go of the ship and dropped the rest of the way into the water.

On the way to the ship, she and Munch had the current to their advantage. Now the current would take her to the pirates and the attacking naval vessels.

Against the current it was. Brigid set out, holding the box above the water with one hand and swimming with her legs and other hand.

All she had to do was get to the nearest shore. Munch and Allen could find her from there.

Behind her, the pirates shouted. More booms, then splintering crashes.

Brigid panted as she fought the current, trying to cut across it as best as she could without being swept around the ship into the open. Foot by foot, she fought her way across the river. Never had she been so happy when her feet squished in the muck of the river bottom. She all but crawled from the river, crouching on her knees in the undergrowth.

As she tried to regain her breath, she set down the box

and slowly opened it. She carefully extracted each of the eight walnuts, checking on the pixie babies.

All of them still seemed to be breathing, but she needed to return them to their mothers as soon as possible. Pixie babies needed flower nectar, not a mother's milk, but who knew if the pirates had bothered to feed them. Not to mention they had been all but smothered in this box.

She placed them in the box but left the lid open as she retreated farther into the forest. When she found a sheltered spot between a large tree and a boulder, she settled down to wait. Allen and Munch were foresters. They would find her.

BRIGID JUMPED AS FIRST MUNCH, then Allen ghosted around the boulder. "Oh, good. You're back. I was beginning to wonder."

Munch rested a hand on her shoulder. "Never in trouble."

"That much trouble." Sometime since she'd last seen him, Allen had swapped his clothing back the other direction so that he wore greens and browns again. "Things got a little interesting for a few moments there, but I snatched the captain before the sailors could snag him."

"We questioned him and got a list of his buyers. He didn't know all their names, so it won't be easy to track them down." Munch grimaced and shared a look with Allen.

"Sophie and I will continue to research and track them down. It's all we can do at this point." Allen hefted his lute. "We left the captain hogtied where the naval authorities will find him as they clean up the pirates."

"At least we won't have to worry about these pirates taking any more pixies." Munch gestured back the way they'd come. "The navy confiscated their ship and rounded up most of them."

"Good." Brigid stood, still clutching the box to her. "Let's get these babies home."

Chapter Three

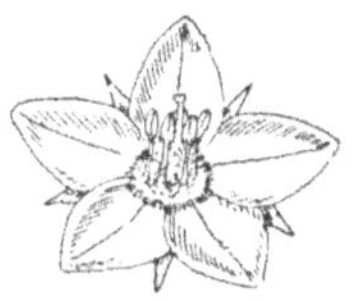

"The Primrose stopped the pirates. They will not steal your children again."

Facing the group of pixie parents who had come to the Court of Knowledge to claim their children, Brigid stuffed back the heat that still burned through her at the thought of what those pirates had been doing. Stealing people from their homes was wrong, whether it was fae stealing humans or humans stealing pixie children to sell as pets to keep in cages.

"The Primrose rescued eight pixie children." Brigid paused as the pixie mothers and fathers shared glances. There were more than eleven sets of parents standing there, hoping for the return of their children. As much as Brigid wished, she could not provide a happy ending for everyone. "The Primrose's allies will continue to search for clues as to the whereabouts of the rest of the children. He cannot promise that they will all be found, but he will not give up trying to find them."

It was the most she could promise.

Brigid reached into the basket she carried, gently picking up one of the walnut shells laid carefully in the padding of sheepskin.

As she held out the walnut shell, one of the pixies raced forward, her eyes wide with hope and tears, and took the walnut shell. She opened it, revealing the tiny baby pixie sleeping inside. Tears spilled down the pixie's face as she hugged the walnut shell close, bobbing a curtsey and mumbling profuse thanks.

The pixie mother returned to her husband and handed over the walnut shell. He cradled it with a reverent, tearful expression of his own.

In a blink, the pixie mother transformed to her small form, a glowing ball of light as tall as Brigid's hand was long. Glittering pixie dust scattered from her as she swooped in, retrieved her baby from the walnut shell, and cradled the infant.

The father transformed too, and the two of them zipped away, the mother with the babe, and the father toting the walnut shell.

One by one, Brigid reached into her basket, pulled out a walnut shell, and held it out to be claimed by the baby's parents.

With each baby that was returned to his or her parents, the faces of the rest of the pixies grew more and more tense, then twisted with grief as they realized their children were likely not among those rescued.

When the last pixie baby had been returned to her parents, Brigid had to take a deep breath and steel herself before facing the remaining pixies.

A few of the mothers were crying. The fathers had tight jaws, their wings buzzing even harder.

"I'm sorry." Brigid's throat closed, her words coming out choked. There was nothing more she could do until Alan and Sophie found more clues as to the whereabouts of the missing pixie children.

After sharing a glance with some of the others still standing there, one pixie woman with vermillion hair and glittering green eyes stepped forward, facing Brigid with a mix of grief and steel. "We know the Primrose is doing his best. He might be hated by many in the Fae Realm, but he is a hero to us. No one else would care about the pixie children."

Their trust was almost too much. A part of her wanted to turn and leave rather than bear the weight of their gaze.

It was far easier, rescuing humans when she rarely met the loved ones in person and didn't have to face their trust or gratitude.

"We created a gift for the Primrose." The pixie held out a basket woven out of daisies.

For a moment, Brigid hesitated. It was always dangerous to accept a gift from a Fae. It could be a trick. It could be a means to put her in debt to them.

Perhaps, these pixies already felt they were in the debt of the Primrose. This was their way of paying that debt back. Nor did Brigid think these pixies—who needed the Primrose's help to find their lost children—would do anything to endanger her or the Primrose.

Brigid took the basket, then peeked inside. Eleven necklaces lay inside. Each necklace had a pendant formed of a flower encased in amber and strung on a nearly invisible string, likely some kind of spider silk expertly prepared and braided by the tiny hands of the pixies. "These are lovely."

They were. But it was a puzzling gift for a Fae hero that these pixies assumed was a man.

"We wished to thank the Primrose for his efforts on our behalf, even if he cannot rescue every child who was stolen." The pixie woman gestured at the basket. "All of us pooled our magic to make these. They create a glamour. It is not as strong as a glamour some of the fae can create, but it's our hope that these will assist the Primrose and his allies in all of their rescues, both of humans and fae."

Brigid hugged the basket to her. This was a great gift, indeed. She would make good use of this, especially since she was a human unable to create a glamour for herself. "On behalf of the Primrose, I thank you for this gift to aid him in all his endeavors."

The remaining pixies gave her solemn nods in return, acknowledging her thanks.

Brigid smiled at the pixie woman, then the other pixies still standing there. "How do the necklaces work?"

"Grip the pendant, think about how you wish to appear, then tuck the pendant beneath your clothing against your skin. When you wish to end the glamour, take the pendant back out so that it is no longer touching you." The pixie motioned to demonstrate as she spoke. "The better, more specific an image you have in your mind, the better the glamour will hold. You can appear as someone else or as someone completely formed from imagination. Unlike a stronger glamour, however, if someone touches you, they will be able to see beneath the glamour. Also, those who know you or the person you are portraying well will also begin to see beneath the glamour, if not peel it away entirely. We apologize that the glamour is not stronger."

"The Primrose will be able to make good use of these,

never fear." Brigid glanced over her shoulder, meeting Munch's gaze.

His mouth tipped into a hint of a smile. Oh, yes. She definitely had a few ideas on how to use these necklaces quite effectively indeed.

ONCE THEY WERE BACK in their House in the Court of Knowledge, Brigid turned to Munch and grinned, holding out the basket. "Are you thinking what I am thinking?"

"Probably not." Munch shrugged, matching her grin with a lopsided one of his own. "What did you have in mind?"

She picked up a handful of necklaces, letting them dangle from her fingers. "If we play this right, we are going to rescue ten or more humans from all across the Fae Realm all in one day. And Lord Chauvlyn is going to help us do it."

Lord Chauvlyn, a lord of the Court of Revels, was the Primrose's nemesis. Even though he had discovered Brigid was the Primrose, he had still been unable to catch her in the act of actually stealing humans away from the fae who had stolen them.

Munch's eyebrows shot up nearly to the widow's peak of his receding hairline as he gaped at her. Then his eyes lit, and his smirk returned. "Now that sounds like fun."

"My thoughts exactly." Brigid smirked and held out one of the necklaces to Munch.

LORD CHAUVLYN SWAGGERED out of the Anywhere Door into the Harvest Court. The Harvest Court guards—a pair of pumpkin-headed creatures dressed in black armor—straightened, then pointed their spears at him.

He waved carelessly, flicking one of the tips of the spears away from him. "I have come to see my old friend Lord Burnt. Surely you won't bar me?"

After a moment, the pumpkin-headed guards lifted their spears and returned to their places.

"Thank you. I doubt I'll be long." Lord Chauvlyn waved as he brushed past them. "I've come to retrieve a gift."

Less than an hour later when Lord Chauvlyn returned with a human female in tow, the guards did not even bother to stop him.

LORD CHAUVLYN STALKED through the passageways of the Court of Stone, then stopped to knock on a door.

It swung open to reveal a fae lord standing there, something about his features sharp, hinting at his other nature—the dragon side. "Yes?"

"That human you have. I wish to purchase it." Lord Chauvlyn dug into his pocket, then pulled out a pouch. He opened it, then poured its contents onto his hand. A few chunks of real gold from the Human Realm glittered on his palm. "I will pay in gold."

The fae dragon shifter's eyes lit up as he swayed forward, almost unconsciously. Gold proved to be a draw to the dragon inside him. "Deal." The dragon shifted reached forward, as if about to snatch the gold from Lord Chauvlyn's hand.

Lord Chauvlyn swiped the gold away before the fae could take it. "You will get the gold once I have the human."

The fae dragon shifter frowned, but he stepped back inside. Moments later he reappeared, a human at his side.

Lord Chauvlyn exchanged the human for the gold, then he was on his way before the dragon shifter realized that the gold he held was really worthless rocks plated in gold.

LORD CHAUVLYN TIPTOED along one of the many bridges that crisscrossed the green goo that formed much of the Swamp Court. He peered into a few of the huts he passed until he found the one he wanted.

Ducking inside, he found a human boy, tied by the ankle to the center post of the hut. The boy was pounding moss into a mush with a mortar and pestle. At Lord Chauvlyn's approach, the boy glanced up, then cowered, arms over his head.

Lord Chauvlyn knelt, then held out a small, red flower. "I am a friend."

The boy blinked at him, then at the wild fae primrose in the fae lord's hand.

When he didn't reach to take it, Lord Chauvlyn dropped the wild fae primrose on the floor, then sliced through the boy's rope.

Once the boy was free, Lord Chauvlyn gently took his arm. The boy's eyes widened, and he gaped up at him.

Lord Chauvlyn smiled, then placed a finger to his mouth.

The boy nodded, then together, they walked through the Swamp Court back to the Anywhere Door.

"WHAT IS THE MEANING OF THIS?" King Oberon bellowed, both because he was angry and because such a volume was necessary to pierce the cacophony of the other shouting fae.

Lord Chauvlyn crossed his arms, glaring from King Oberon to the crowd of fae, which seemed to be growing by the moment. Lord Burnt from the Harvest Court had been the first to arrive, claiming that Lord Chauvlyn had stolen a human from him. Then a dragon shifter from the Court of Stone. Then more fae, from the Swamp Court, Court of Lakes, Court of Islands, and more. All claiming that Lord Chauvlyn had marched into their court and stolen away a human.

"I had nothing to do with this." Lord Chauvlyn scowled and gestured at the milling crowd of angry fae. "I am barred from using the Anywhere Doors. I couldn't possibly have been in all of these courts in the past few hours."

"Then how do you explain this?" King Oberon stomped his foot as he jabbed a hand at the fae, the force of the motion jiggling his substantial paunch.

Lord Chauvlyn opened his mouth, but before he could answer, another fae scurried into the room, glanced around, then shoved through the crowd until he reached the fae lord. Lord Chauvlyn whirled on him. "What? Let me guess. You had a human stolen from you, and you claim I did it."

"No, my lord." The fae blinked at him, as if he couldn't quite believe what he was seeing, as he held out a folded piece of paper. "I have a message. From you, sir. You told me to give it to you."

Lord Chauvlyn snatched the paper, then opened it, and read the note inside.

Hey diddle diddle,
Oh, what a riddle,

The frog jumped over the thistle.
Oh, what a rhyme,
Too many Chauvlyns at a time.
The Wild Fae Primrose wrote this epistle.

Lord Chauvlyn could not help the growl in the back of his throat as he crumpled the paper in his fist.

The Primrose. Brigid.

For a moment, the memory of her solemn face as she walked away when she could have ordered his death, flashed through his mind.

Then he shook it away. She was his enemy, no matter the mercy she had given him.

He would catch her someday. No matter what it took. And then he would make her pay for every taunting word.

Free Ebook!

Thanks so much for reading *Wild Fae Primrose*! I hope Munch and Brigid made you laugh, even if you were shaking your head at their awkward romance! If you loved the book, please consider leaving a review on Amazon or Goodreads. Reviews help your fellow readers find books that they will love.

If you ever find typos in any of my books, feel free to email me at taragrayce(at)taragrayce(dot)com.

If you sign up for my newsletter, you'll also receive the free novella *Steal a Swordmaiden's Heart.*

This novella tells the story of how King Theseus of the Court of Knowledge won the hand of Hippolyta, Queen of the Swordmaidens.

If you don't wish to sign up for my newsletter, Steal a Swordmaiden's Heart is available on Amazon, though it isn't in KU like the rest of the series.

Sign up for my newsletter now

NIGHT OF SECRETS

Love is a distraction when the Library is on the line.

Despite being humans living in the Fae Realm, Viola, along with her brother Sebastian, have achieved their dream to become librarians and establish their own outpost library in the Court of Islands. When an attack on their way to the outpost separates them, Viola arrives alone, not knowing if Sebastian is alive or dead.

To preserve their dream and investigate what went wrong, Viola uses a fae glamour to be both herself and her brother. She didn't count on falling for the island's handsome fae ruler, Lord Orsino. But he's in love with Olivia—the same fae lady who Sebastian had been courting. Too bad everything only gets more complicated from there.

Can Viola navigate this tangled web of love to save the outpost library and find her brother? Or will an old enemy threaten not just Viola and the outpost but also the Great Library itself?

Inspired by Shakespeare's *Twelfth Night*, this standalone fae fantasy romance features fae rom-com hilarity, a girl in disguise, and a magical fae library, perfect for fans of K.M. Shea, Sylvia Mercedes, and Sarah K.L. Wilson.

Preorder on Kindle Today!

If you missed the previous adventures and would like to read more about Basil & Meg or Guy & Robin, pick up *Stolen Midsummer Bride* and *Bluebeard and the Outlaw*!

Stolen Midsummer Bride

Steal a bride. Save the library. Try not to die.

Basil, a rather scholarly fae, works as an assistant librarian at the Great Library of the Court of Knowledge. Lonely and unwilling to join the yearly Midsummer Revel to find a mate, Basil takes the advice of his talking horse companion and decides to steal a human bride instead.

Bluebeard and the Outlaw

Marriage: the ultimate heist.

Robin of the Greenwood spends her days robbing from the rich to feed the poor. When Robin discovers the Duke Guy "Bluebeard" plans to marry again, she conceives a plan for a final, big score. The lord is notorious for

killing his wives, but Robin has no plans to be dead wife number four.

Forest of Scarlet

The fae snatch humans as playthings to torment. The Primrose steals them back.

Vowing that no other family would endure the same fear and pain she felt when her older sister was snatched by the fae, Brigid puts on an empty-headed façade while she rescues humans in the shadowy guise of the Primrose, hero to humans, bane to the fae. Her only regret is that she can't tell the truth to Munch, the young man in the human realm who she's trying very hard not to fall in love with.

Will this stolen bride's sister and Robin Hood's brother reveal the truth of their hearts before the Fae Realm snatches hope away from them forever?

Acknowledgments

I hope you enjoyed *Wild Fae Primrose*! This story started out as the beginning of *Forest of Scarlet*, but I soon realized there was too much here for a short prologue (Ha. Short. Who was I kidding?). So I broke these stories into a separate prequel, which bridges the gap in time between *Stolen Midsummer Bride* and *Bluebeard and the Outlaw* and sets up Munch and Brigid's relationship (or lack of one) for *Forest of Scarlet*.

Also, I realized in the writing of this prequel that I made the classic writing mistake of picking too many names that all started with the same letter (namely, the letter B). Since the previous books were already published, I was stuck and couldn't change any of them. Apologies for that. Luckily, by the time we get to *Forest of Scarlet*, Buddy, Basil, and Brigid don't have too many scenes where they are all together. So if you found the climax of the first story in this prequel a tad confusing for that reason, it will get better in the first book. Promise.

Thanks so much once again for picking up one of my books! Your support is the reason I can keep writing and publishing, and each sale and review means so much!

As always, special thanks to everyone who made this book possible. My family: my dad, my mom, my brothers, and my sisters-in-law. My friends: Bri, Paula, Jill. My writing friends: Molly, Morgan, Addy, Savannah, Sierra, and many others. My proofreaders: Tom, Mindy, Tessa, and Deborah. All of you guys are the best team an author could ask for!

Also by Tara Grayce

<u>**World of Elven Alliance / Alliance Kingdoms**</u>

ELVEN ALLIANCE

Fierce Heart

War Bound

Death Wind

Troll Queen

Pretense

Shield Band

Elf Prince

Heart Bond

Elf King

WAR OF THE ALLIANCE

Wings of War

Stalk the Sky

Fly to Fury

<u>Tales of the Fae Realm</u>

COURT OF MIDSUMMER MAYHEM

Stolen Midsummer Bride

Steal a Swordmaiden's Heart

Forest of Scarlet

Wild Fae Primrose

Night of Secrets

A VILLAIN'S EVER AFTER

Bluebeard and the Outlaw

SACRIFICED HEARTS

Mountain of Dragons and Sacrifice

Of Dragons and Stone

TETHERED HEARTS

Ties of Bargains

<u>Middle Grade</u>

PRINCESS BY NIGHT

Lost in Averell

* 9 7 8 1 9 4 3 4 4 2 3 6 2 *